LOCKI FEMINIZATION

2

No escape for a feminized sissy

Lady Alexa

Copyright © Lady Alexa 2020
1st Edition

All rights reserved. No reproduction, copy or transmission of this publication or section in this publication may be reproduced, copied or transmitted without written permission of the author.

This novel is a work of fiction. Names, characters, businesses, places, events and incidents are either the products of the author's imagination or used in a fictitious manner. Any resemblance to actual persons, living or dead, or actual events is purely coincidental.

This novel contains explicit scenes of a sexual nature including forced male to female gender transformation, female domination, humiliation, CFNM, spanking and reluctant feminisation. All characters in this story are aged 18 and over.

Strictly for adults aged 18 and over or the age of maturity in your country.

Subscribe to my blog charting my real-life FLR and forced feminisation lifestyle with my feminised husband Alice here:

www.ladyalexauk.com

You can also subscribe to my newsletter and receive special offers, free articles and stories. Go to www.ladyalexauk.com and enter your email address into the newsletter box in the sidebar.

CONTENTS

1. **Boychick**

2. **Femdom pupils**

3. **Sissy girl**

4. **The messages**

5. **Sissy schoolgirl**

6. **Sissy photo shoot**

7. **The call**

8. **A change of plan**

9. **The journey**

10. **Uncovered**

11. **A foam bath**

12. **Pretty in pink**

13. **The calling**

14. **It's the police**

15. **The surprise package**

16. **Out of the frying pan**

1 – Boychik

David wore a pink satin maid's dress with a small white apron at the front. The dress had white starched petticoats which flared out like a ballerina's tutu.

The maid's dress was too short to cover his panties; the hard outline of his barred metal cock cage was visible. His dress wasn't a proper working maid's dress, it was too impractical for that. It was a statement of his role and position in the household. Ms Louise Lipman liked it that way.

David Amey's life had changed beyond recognition since he had started working at this remote renovated farmhouse in the depths of the

English countryside. He had started work as the personal assistant for Ms J L Ryder, the world-famous author. He was no longer her personal assistant. Ms Ryder had demoted him to a feminised cleaner and waitress thanks to Ms Ryder's friend, Ellen.

Today Louise Lipman, Ms Ryder's agent, had reduced him further in status. He was now the sissy maid for the all-female household. The two women had taken advantage of the Coronavirus lockdown and the fact he had no money and nowhere else to go. It was a perfect storm for David.

He walked to his full-length mirror hanging on the back of his bedroom door. He made tiny delicate unbalanced steps in four-inch heels. It was the only way he could walk in these shoes. His shoes were white with ankle straps and thin heels. He felt as if he were moving across the room on tip-toes. The balls of his feet were going to ache after a short time working in these shoes. They hadn't put him in working clothes, although he was expected to work in them. These were sissy clothes and they served a different purpose.

Ellen, Ms Ryder's personal assistant and friend, had padlocked the high-heeled shoes to his ankles and the metal cock cage to his penis and balls. She did this with relish following the instructions of Ms Louise Lipman. Both Ellen and Ms Lipman had the keys for the cage and shoes; they kept them on a chain around their necks. Flaunted around their necks would be more accurate.

How had things come to this? He was dressed like a fool, no real woman ever wore clothes like this. What was it they wanted from this humiliation? And why? He never understood the ways of these women. They wanted him feminised, but not exactly as them. An extreme parody.

He had to ensure he was perfectly presented before returning downstairs to serve the four ladies. They were waiting for him to serve afternoon tea for the first time as their sissy maid. Ms Lipman set a series of rules for him to follow. She said she would punish him for the slightest error, however small. It was as if she enjoyed spanking him in front of the other ladies. Panties down, over her knee. Sometimes with her hand, other times with a wooden spoon.

He looked in at his face in the mirror to check he had complied with every instruction Ms Lipman had relayed via Ellen. Bright red lipstick, freshly applied with no smudges: check. Light honey-blond hair, styled thick and wavy, no grey roots: check. Pink bow, tied at the back of his hair, large and extravagant, both bows exactly six inches in diameter: check. Long false eyelashes attached: check. Large hoop earrings clipped on: check. He inspected his hands: long false nails, pink and glossy, no chipped ends, none loose: check.

He turned his back to the mirror and looked over the puffy shoulders of his dress. Seams straight on the black fish-net stockings: check. He turned back. 38C breast forms level under his bra: check.

He was ready. He walked out of his attic bedroom, made for the top stair and steadied himself on the bannister. It was tricky getting down on four-inch stilettos. He heard the bell tinkling from below, the mistresses were ringing, getting impatient. He was taking too long. This could only mean one thing. Punishment.

He staggered down the steps, one foot at a time as he grasped the bannister, his knuckles white. The bell tinkled again and a burst of anger rose in him. He had to suppress that emotion, it would do him no good.

He made it to the bottom stair and hesitated a moment. This was his grand unveiling as a full-time live-in sissy maid. He walked towards the kitchen area, his heels clicking on the tiled floor of the hallway. It was the first time the four ladies would see him in his new sissy-maid dress.

Giggles flowed from the kitchen. They had heard his clicking heels and his petticoat rustles and crinkles when he walked. He adjusted his dress for no good reason, it wasn't going to get any longer than it was. Ms Lipman hadn't chosen one too short by accident. He took a deep breath as he stopped by the open doorway. More giggling, they knew he was there.

There was no sense delaying any further, it was time he went in. Time to get it over with. In time they would get used to him this way, he supposed. He took another breath. It was better to show confidence, pretend it was fine to look like a pansy girl.

It might reduce his humiliation if they thought he wasn't bothered. His legs turned to jelly and his stomach was twisted tight like twine.

He clopped into the kitchen, heels clipping against the floor tiles, his head held high. He pulled a fake expression and tried to stop his legs trembling. Loud laughter greeted him instantly. It was his arch tormentor, Ellen, and her young niece, Jenny. He looked down, stopped and curtsied, as per Ms Lipman's earlier instructions. Jenny's laughter rose to a screech; her childishness irritated him.

David's penis grew hard into the cock cage. For reasons he couldn't begin to understand, Jenny's amusement made him excited. He hated that and was glad he had panties on. And he was glad he had the cock cage which held in his embarrassment.

Ms Ryder sat cool and detached at the table, her legs crossed elegantly. She wore dark wide trousers and a cashmere sweater. Her long ponytail was tied back tightly in her long dark hair.

Ellen, David's nemesis, looked triumphant. She had started this humiliation in an attempt to have her niece Jenny take over his job.

Jenny was in tears of laughter. Her long blond hair hung over large breasts, held tightly in a top that looked a size too small. He guessed that at eighteen, there was more growth in them yet. She wore a short white ra-ra skirt and her strong legs were bare. She was attractive despite being stocky.

Finally, his new mistress, Louise Lipman. She was the eldest of the group, touching fifty, he guessed. She had her glasses perched on the end of her nose with a thin metal chain attached to the arms and looped around her neck. She peered through slitted eyes at her new submissive sissy maid.

"Come here, Amy," she said. It was what they all called him now, a female first name based on his surname: Amey.

David walked towards her, conscious of his penis bursting against the bars of his cock cage. He did not understand the excitement of the situation which was awful, humiliating and degrading.

"Who told you to put panties on?" Ms Lipman stared him hard in the eyes. "Boychik."

He avoided her stare and picked at the ends of his long hair with both hands. "Boychik?" he mumbled.

Ms Lipman smiled, waiting on his reply.

"I assumed I should wear panties, Mistress. My dress doesn't cover me."

"Oy. Don't assume, my dear. Didn't you think I might want your little caged clitty on show?" Ms Lipman shook her head and looked at the other women. "It's small and cute and I think everyone should see what a boychik you are.

David's throat closed. There it was again. Boychik. This was getting worse and downhill fast. His attempts to be confident were falling around his shaved legs.

Ms Lipman had a point, he wasn't that big down below. There was no need to rub it in by exhibiting it and pointing it out, that wasn't fair.

Yet at the same time something in what she was doing and saying about his penis grabbed at his stomach and tingled like electricity in his groin. As did the word boychik.

"Never mind, I have an idea." Ms Lipman pointed towards the kitchen drawers. "Jenny, darling, would you be a dear and pass me a sharp knife?"

Jenny's eyebrows furrowed in a look of intrigue. She jumped up to rummage in the drawer, boobs bouncing loosely under her tight top. She wasn't wearing a bra. This made it all the worse for David's excitement. She found a small sharp knife and brought it over to Ms Lipman.

David took a step back, causing more laughter from Jenny and Ellen.

"Come here, Amy, I'm not going to hurt you."

David stepped forward again, his petticoats rustled. The front of his panties was six inches from Ms Lipman's face.

She turned to the other women, the knife held high in her hand, pointing to the ceiling. "I've found over the years of training and managing boychiks, like Amy, that one secret to their continued submission is the exposure and humiliation of their little clitties. Keeping their little clitties on show makes them silly and malleable. It's strange, but it's an effective control mechanism."

David did not understand what she meant; this was the first time he had ever been in a situation like this one. He was in uncharted territory.

Ms Lipman turned back to him and pressed the knife tip against the front of his panties and held them out a little with her free hand. She cut a slit up the front and pushed it back over his cock cage. The panties framed his cock cage, his failing erection pressed against the metal bars. This led to more howls of laughter from Ellen and Jenny. Ms Ryder observed the situation calmly, detached; David was unable to gauge her reactions. One thing he did know, she wasn't going to step in to stop his humiliation and degradation. She was more concerned with her writing than anything that happened to him.

That was what had caused this feminisation problem in the first place. If it was a problem.

"Her little clitty is hard against the metal bars. How cute, she's excited," Ellen said.

David cowered, his shoulders hunched. He wanted to run or disappear in the deepest hole possible. Ellen and Jenny peered in closer to look at his cock cage. Jenny poked a long pink fingernail through the bars to press his penis. David's heart beat hard against his chest; he wiped a bead of sweat away from his forehead with the back of a hand.

Ms Lipman continued with her lesson on sissy control. "As you can see, she is in a state of high excitement, but with no chance of release. By that I mean ejaculation."

Ms Ryder shook her head at her agent, Ms Lipman, as if to say *you're naughty*.

"This gives us greater control over the little boychik dearies, their emotional senses are overwhelmed and in a constant state of high exhilaration." Ms Lipman sat back like a lawyer making her case. "They are such schmucks, but there you have it."

"This is funny." Jenny said. "Can I take a photo, Louise? I want to send it to my *besties*." Jenny brought out her phone and held it to him.

David knew that besties meant best friends and this was not good news. He'd soon be all over the internet. Again.

Ms Lipman waved a hand and nodded. "Boychiks love their photos being taken and shared. They pretend they don't, but they do. It makes them gooey with desire for others to see them as their true feminine selves. The little dearies."

David wanted to flee. He did not want a photo shared on social media of him dressed like this, Louise Lipman had got that wrong. Surely. There was nowhere to go though, he couldn't escape this sissy nightmare. Or was that boychick? He couldn't leave the house dressed in a pink dress that was too short. Besides, the country was in COVID lockdown and he'd be stopped by the police. That would not be a good situation. Arrested by the police for being outside in an offensive sissy maid's dress.

Jenny clicked a couple of longer shots of him in the dress and a couple of close-ups of his cock cage. She concentrated on pressing the screen on her phone, a tongue poking out. He assumed she was sending the photos to her friends, her *besties*. Jenny irritated him with her infantile style of speaking and behaviour. Her evident excitement at his situation made him feel all the more weak and exhilarated. That was a feeling he was trying to suppress. It didn't make sense.

Was he enjoying this? It was too much to think about.

2 – Femdom pupils

Before he could think about his question, Ms Lipman spoke. "Boychiks love the exposure of their precious little clitties. This means they are ours to do with as we wish, because it's what they want too. Control the clitty, control the sissy boychick, that's my motto." Ms Lipman considered what she had said. "I have a few other mottos, such as: Put them in pretty dresses, give them girl's names, humiliate them. There are a few others, but you get the point."

Ellen and Jenny were listening with rapt attention to Ms Lipman: two pupils for the new teacher. A teacher in enforced feminisation.

"Amy, make us all tea, we're waiting." Ellen waved him away with a dismissive flourish of her hand.

Ms Ryder got up. "Bring mine to my office, Amy, I need to start on my next book. I don't have time to watch the show," She left the kitchen without a glance at David.

David scurried to fill the kettle and prepare the tea. He had to ask the big question while he worked: Why did Louise Lipman want him dressed in this way? She had dressed him as a parody of a real girl. She had made it plain he wasn't a real girl when she started to call him boychik.

Ellen had put him in female clothing before Ms Lipman had arrived. She had gone a step further, dressing him in an exaggerated pink maid's dress and heels that were too high to walk in with ease. No real woman would wear these clothes and they were impractical for the role she wanted him to perform. It would have been easier in flat shoes and a pair of trousers, or at least a practical black cotton skirt. He had become accustomed to that, before Ms Lipman changed the rules.

The kettle boiled and David poured the water into a teapot. It was time to ask, time to understand why she was doing this to him. "Ms Lipman, may I ask a question?"

The animated conversation between Louise, Ellen and Jenny stopped sharply. Ellen got up to move towards him. Louise put a hand on her arm.

"It's OK, Ellen. Let Amy say what she has to say before we punish her. It might be interesting and also informative for you."

Her? Ms Lipman's use of the female pronoun grated on his nerves. The trouble was he had that feeling again, that tingle that started in his stomach and reached down to his penis when the ladies called him by a female pronoun. He stood straight in a vain attempt to show gravitas. Impossible in this dress, he thought, and he slumped back.

"Ms Lipman," he started. "Why do you want me dressed this way? I'm like a cartoon vision of a girl. Can't I wear plainer clothes? I don't mind working here for you all, I'll wear a skirt and flat female shoes if you want me to. But please, can I change into a plain skirt?"

She watched him, her eyebrows raised in amused interest. "Don't be ridiculous. I'm pleased you want to wear a skirt. But no, you can't change. I like you like this. You're not a real woman, so why would I put you in normal female clothes?"

"Why do you want me looking like this?" he asked.

Ellen and Jenny looked at Louise. Louise smiled an indulgent grin.

"It's simple. I prefer males in pretty sissy clothing. I believe males are better as boychiks.

And it's intoxicating for me, the power and control, the ability to do as I please with you." She thought for a moment. "I think the real question here is why you love it."

David spluttered. What was she talking about? He didn't love this, he hated it. He had no choice. Was she crazy?

"I don't love it, I'd prefer to go back to how I was. A man."

Louise threw her head back and laughed out loud. "I don't think you were ever a man in the sense of being masculine. Ellen told me you turned up wearing a female suit and with long blond hair in a female style. When I arrived here, you were dressed in a tiny skirt with a mass of blond hair and you ejaculated over my shoes."

She rested her chin on a fist. "So you see, you were always a boychik."

David's face dropped. This conversation was becoming uncomfortable. She had a point.

Ms Lipman continued, "Tell me why you haven't fought back. Why you haven't complained or fought back in any way. You could have gone back to London? I hear a lot of excuses, but you love this and we've given you the excuse to be a sissy boychik. Isn't that what's going on?"

Heat burned at his cheeks. He hung his head. This wasn't true. It was easy for her to say he could have complained or run away. He couldn't. Where would he run to in sissy clothes? He would be homeless and in girls' clothes.

Impossible. He was trapped here. Ms Lipman was playing with him.

"I see the cat's got your tongue now, Amy," Louise said, amused. "Serve us that tea and be a good girly sissy. I want no more silly questions."

Defeated, he poured the tea and served it to the ladies. He took a cup out to Ms Ryder. Her office door was open and he knocked and went in. He placed the cup on her desk and backed away. Ms Ryder took no notice of him as she typed intently on her laptop. She didn't notice he hadn't curtsied, or wasn't bothered. He liked her indifference. What was happening to him?

David returned to the kitchen. Ms Lipman rolled a finger, her reminder to curtsey when he entered a room. He curtseyed and waited.

She took a sip of her tea and placed the cup back on the saucer on the kitchen table. She held a chrome-like metal device in one hand, the domed centre glinted and caught the light from the window. The device was about six-inches long with a flange at one end and the domed bulge in the middle.

"Bend over my knee, Amy."

What was this? Now what was going on? He bent over her knee and she pulled down the back of his panties. He heard her unclip a lid. There was an odd sensation around his anus, like cold slime. He felt her work her fingers around his bum hole and he relaxed. This sensation was unexpected and pleasant. There was an instant of sharp pain. A cold and smooth feeling burned inside him. His anus felt full.

Ms Lipman pulled his panties back onto his bum, adjusted the open area around his cock cage and pushed him away. The feeling of being full inside was strange. His buttocks were slightly apart from whatever she had put inside him.

"Do you see ladies?" She addressed Ellen and Jenny. "No fight when I placed the butt plug in her behind. She enjoys being humiliated." She wore a self-satisfied expression pasted across her face. "As for you, Amy, you'll be wearing this butt plug all day and evening and you're only allowed to remove it for bed. Or other necessities of course."

He stammered, "What? What?"

She told him to be quiet and turned to her two fascinated pupils. "Ladies, the next part of this project is to widen her anus substantially and to reduce the size of her clitty."

"Ms Lipman...," he started to complain.

"Shut up, Amy." Ms Lipman's voice was sharp and angry. "Don't be such a whinnying schmuck." She continued addressing her pupils. "We will regularly increase the size of her butt plug until she can accept much bigger things in there."

Big things? What was she talking about, big things? He didn't want a wide anus or *big things* in there.

"At the same time, we will be reducing the size of her clitty cage week on week until we have reduced her little clitty to less than an inch long." She smiled. "So it becomes small, pretty and girly."

His whole body flowed hot at her words. This was going beyond dressing and hairstyles. This was too far. "Ms Lipman, you can't make physical changes to me. It's not right. I don't want a smaller penis or bigger anus hole."

She made her familiar eyebrow raise. "Oh, Amy, you are such a putz at times, it's not up to you. These changes are only the beginning. I have a whole lot more planned for you." She reflected for a moment. "You're a piece of clay for me to shape and mould. Think of me as the sculptor."

David's mouth dropped open.

3 – Sissy girl

David sat on the side of his bed, his bare feet on the floor. It was a little after nine, but Ms Lipman said that good sissy boychiks should have early nights.

His leg muscles ached from wearing the high heels. His chest ached from having his masculinity emasculated. The humiliation wasn't over, Ellen was standing over him, arms crossed. She had forced him to put on a baby-doll nightie which was pink and with frills. The nightie didn't cover him when he stood so sitting was preferable.

Ellen had his open cock cage in her hand. She began twirling it around a finger as her lips pursed in thought. "Louise wants you milked tonight before I put the cage back on. It won't be a regular occasion as you'll be in chastity most of the time. She feels it will be useful to associate sexual release with your pretty sissy clothes and your admission you want to become a girl."

David listened, wondering what was coming next. Ellen bent over and pulled his nightie up and wrapped the frills around his intense erection. This caused it to strain more. His penis was wrapped in pink, the end protruding from the mass of frills surrounding it. He was desperate to cum and he guessed it wouldn't take much.

"Rub the end of your little clitty with your fingers. Keep it wrapped with the frills and repeat; *I am a naughty sissy girl, I am a naughty sissy girl.* Keep saying this until you cum."

David looked at her. Was she crazy? His hesitation resulted in a slap across his face.

"Do it now, stupid girl."

He rubbed his red swollen penis end and repeated. "*I am a naughty sissy girl, I am a naughty sissy girl.*" This was crazy.

The feelings of ejaculation zinged into his penis and stomach.

"Good girl, keep going. And cum into this." Ellen handed him a mug.

He guessed that made sense, he didn't want to make a mess on the rug or on his nightie otherwise.

"I am a sissy girl. I am a sissy girl. I am a sissy girl."

This was wonderful. He wanted to delay cumming for a while, the feelings were intense and he didn't want them to end.

"I am a sissy girl, I am a sissy girl, I am a sissy girl."

"Good girl, good girl, keep going. I want you milked and empty"

"I'm a sissy girl," he panted. "I'm a sissy... girl. I'm... A... Sissy."

His cum burst into the mug like a rifle shot.

"Sissy. Girl. I'm."

It kept coming and coming. He fell forward over the mug. The sweet salty smell of his cum rose through his nostrils. That was incredible, such a release. Waves of elation flooded over him, his shoulders dropped in relaxation, his mind was free and light. He forgot where he was or who was watching. Everything went into the release, the satisfaction.

"Drink it all like a good girl." Ellen's sharp voice dragged him from his pleasure.

He struggled to take in what she had said. He squeezed the last drops from his soft penis. The waves of pleasure receded fast.

"I told you to...," She breathed out hard and slow. "Drink it."

He recoiled from the mug, holding it out from his body. Ellen took the mug of cum from his light grip and pushed it to his mouth.

"Drink it."

He recoiled again, disgusted. His mouth shut tight and firm. The smell wafted towards him, invading his nose, pushing into his eyes.

Ellen kept it at his mouth. "You will drink it, girl. Louise wants you to get used to drinking cum. She wants you to enjoy the taste and smell. You're going to be swallowing plenty in the future, she told me."

He glared at her. What was she talking about? He was never going to be drinking lots of cum. How would that ever happen?

Ellen pushed the mug hard into his clamped teeth, the damp salty smell stronger and more dank closer to his nostrils. He shivered. She clamped a thumb and forefinger on his nose to restrict his breathing. He opened his mouth with a squeal. Ellen tipped the viscous cum into his mouth and the tart salty flavour assaulted his tongue. His taste buds stung. Ellen held his mouth open as the last drop dripped onto his tongue like thick glue. She put the mug down and clamped his mouth shut, her hand on his nostrils. He gagged, swallowed and shivered.

Ellen stood away. "Time to go to sleep, sissy girl. Tomorrow I'll have another outfit for you to wear: the school girl. You're going to look cute." Ellen stared hard at him waiting for his reaction. When he didn't say anything, she continued. "We want to try several looks on you, all of them girly and sissy."

Ellen knelt by him and pushed his nightie up to expose his soft penis. She clamped the cock cage around it again and locked it tight. She inspected it for a while, not happy.

"Your clitty cage is already too big."

David looked down. The end of his penis touched against the end of the cage. "It fits fine, Mistress Ellen."

"Yes it does, that's the problem."

Ellen saw his look of confusion. "It needs to be more restrictive."

"I don't understand, Mistress."

David slid into bed, pulling the covers to his chin, he wanted Ellen to go away so he could get privacy. That was in short supply at present.

"Louise has said she wants your clitty much smaller. I need to restrict the room it has inside so it atrophies."

"What? Atrophies" he gulped. He felt weak. David had thought Louise had been talking tough but didn't mean it: she had every intention of shrinking his penis. He couldn't think what the reason might be.

"Yes, that means get smaller. We have a selection of cages for you. I'll put you in the next size down now."

He sat up, flustered. "That's too small."

Satisfaction spread over Ellen's face. "Exactly, about an inch too short. I'll need to squeeze it in. But don't worry, over time it will shrink down to fit. Then we'll take it down in size again."

He pushed himself down into the covers. He wanted her to go away more than anything. Shrink his penis? Were they mad? Why would they want to do this to him? He didn't mind serving them, but this was something else.

Ellen watched him for a moment, she grunted. "I'll get it now."

She left the room and it was as if a dark cloud had left with her. She returned several minutes later with the new cage. She removed the old one and squeezed his flaccid penis into the new one. He squealed as she pushed it in and clipped it shut. She stepped back to admire her work.

The cage was awful. His penis was squashed and folded into the cage.

Ellen folded her arms. "That should do the trick. In a week or two I'll take it down another inch. Or two."

David pulled at the cage, trying to get his penis comfortable. "Take it off, it's too tight."

"Stop fiddling, sissy. I'll remove it in a week to measure progress."

She turned and left. This was not good.

4 – The message

He snuggled under the covers, he wanted sleep to come to obscure the humiliation of the afternoon. He pulled and prodded his cock cage and found a position for his squeezed penis. It wasn't good. It would have to do.

He heard a ping sound. His eyes flicked open. His phone lay on the bedside cabinet, the screen lit. Who the hell would be contacting him? He had no friends or family.

He sat up and took the phone: unknown number. He opened the message.

"Is this Mr David Amey?"

It had been a while since anyone had called him Mr or David. His finger hovered over the screen keyboard. Who on Earth would be contacting him at 10pm at night? Who would be contacting him at any time? And this person wasn't sure it was him. It had to be a scam text? Maybe he'd get lots of spam messages? Maybe calls from people trying to sell him insurance? Or someone saying he'd had a car accident and they could help get compensation?

On the other hand, it was intriguing. He decided to answer.

He typed. "*Im David Amey whose this.*" It felt odd to call himself David again, especially when wearing a frilly baby-doll nightie and a cock cage.

He flicked off the phone's sound. He didn't want Mistress Louise or Ellen taking his phone away. He had lost all other privileges, but they had forgotten, or were not worried, about his phone.

He watched his screen. It lit up.

"I'm sorry it's late, we've had trouble tracking you down Mr Amey."

Tracking him down? Why would anyone want to track him down? His eyes fixed on his title *Mr* Amey. It felt unusual after being referred to as a girl for the past few weeks.

Another message arrived.

"My name is Jennifer Strong of Arbuthnot, Willis and Strong. We are Family Solicitors representing Ms Ruth Amey."

He stared hard at the screen. Ruth Amey? Who the hell was she? He racked his brain. His parents had died fifteen years ago; he was an only son. He never knew his grandparents. His parents hadn't mixed with any family. Was this Ruth Amey a distant relation? He didn't remember her name. There had been no Ruth Amey in his life he was aware of.

Another text came in.

"I need to speak to you regarding Ms Amey. May I call tomorrow? What time is best for you Mr Amey?"

This was odd. A text message at 10pm from a law firm representing someone with the same surname as him. It wouldn't do any harm to speak to Jennifer Strong.

But when would he be free to talk? Mistress Louise allowed him spare time in the early evening for an hour to shower, freshen his make-up, do his hair and to change into a different outfit for his evening work. 6pm should be fine. Make it 6.15 to be sure.

He typed back his reply. *"You can call me at cwarter passed 6."*

Should he tell Mistress Louise? No, it's probably best not to. She didn't like him having outside contacts; this was one of her attractions for him as her personal maid: He had no friends or family. She wanted his entire focus on what she wanted. No, he would keep this call secret.

He lay back down and pulled the covers to his chin. There had been a lot going on. His new outfits as Mistress Louise's maid, Ellen making him masturbate and having to drink it. Disgusting. This message from Jennifer Strong. And Ruth Amey? Who the hell was she? His mind refused to close down, it turned over the events.

Sleep didn't come easy. When it did, it was light with dreams of being a girl with a micro skirt, enormous breasts and having a real vagina. Mistress Louise and Mistress Ellen were pointing and laughing at him. Jenny was taking photos of his open vagina with his legs wide apart like a porn photo. It was a long restless night.

5 – Sissy schoolgirl

David woke with the feeling he was being watched. He rubbed at his sleep-encrusted eyes and opened them. Ellen was standing in his room, a stainless steel cock cage swinging on one finger, her other hand on a hip, one knee bent. David woke instantly.

"New day, new sissy," she said. "Up you get. Baby-doll off, in the shower and I have a new clitty cage for you." Ellen swung it around her finger again, her grin widening.

David dragged himself out of bed, another day of humiliation. He slipped off his baby doll and his penis rammed hard against his cock cage.

Ellen put on a fake face of concern. "Oh dear, does your little miss clitty want to get hard again? Such a shame, sissy girl." She pointed the way to the shower, lips tight.

He went in and showered and shaved while Ellen watched. He dried himself on the large soft and warm pink towel. Ellen beckoned him into the bedroom again.

"Nasty male face shaving, Louise wants to do something about that. Girlies don't shave their faces, do they?"

David scowled. She rewarded his insolence with a slap across the face.

"Sissies like you shouldn't need to shave their faces. Should they." It was a statement but she expected an answer.

David looked to the floor in shame. "No Mistress."

"That's better, girl."

Ellen pulled him towards her by his cock cage. She unlocked it and his penis fell out with a sense of freedom. It was short-lived. Ellen dropped his previous cage to the floor and rammed his semi-erect penis into the one she had been twirling. She clamped it tight around the base of his balls and stood back to admire her work.

David touched it. His penis was folded tight in the much smaller cage. It was smaller than the one she had put on last night. Uncomfortable.

Ellen nodded. "Excellent. Soon it will shrink to the size of the cage and we'll put it in a smaller one. What fun. The other one was much too big."

"But, Mistress Ellen, I don't want a smaller one. The other one was already too small."

He should have expected the slap. It stung his cheek.

"We want you with a tiny tiny clitty. Minuscule. The smaller the better."

Ellen looked at his cramped penis in the cage for a moment and went over to his wardrobe. He hadn't noticed the clothes hanging on the handle of his wardrobe. A wide flared short pleated skirt in a black and white tartan. A white blouse hung behind it.

Ellen grinned again. "Today you'll be a pretty sissy schoolgirl. One inch-wide heeled black shoes and long white socks." Ellen folded her arms and squeezed herself in a cuddle. "I can't wait to see how you look, cute and sissy. This is such fun."

David looked in horror at the clothes. A maid was bad, but now they wanted him dressed as a twelve-year-old girl. What else was there to wear, the maid's dress? He walked to the outfit. He took the skirt off the hanger and held it to him. It was too short. Again.

"Can I wear panties today please, Mistress?" He pleaded.

"No, hurry up, you have work to do. Serving us breakfast and cleaning. Plus I have tutoring to give you. How to sit like a girl, how to walk and wiggle your cute little bum to attract the boys. Oh this is such fun, I'm so pleased Louise came to stay."

David pulled up the elasticated waisted skirt. As he feared, the bottom of his cock cage hung below the hem. He lowered his head, his eyes to the floor, avoiding Ellen's. Ellen passed him a white bra and he clipped it around his chest without looking up. Ellen pushed the breast inserts inside. She giggled.

"38C breasts today. One day I hope you won't need breast inserts."

He nodded, thinking it would be great not to have to wear these inserts. What did she mean he won't need them?"

Ellen shoved the blouse at him before he could ask the question. He put the blouse on. It was a slim fitting top. He let it hang over the skirt, it almost covered it.

"No, no, that won't do," said Ellen. "We need to see your pretty school skirt."

David looked down. "I don't know why, Mistress, it's too short, there's not much of it."

Ellen clapped her hands together. "Yes, I know, isn't that wonderful?"

David thought not, but didn't reply. Her response would have been another slap across his face.

Ellen walked to him and undid the bottom buttons of the blouse and tied the lower part in a knot below his chest. Now his stomach area showed bare. Ellen admired her work with a small nod and pursed lips.

She passed him a pair of white socks. He pulled them over his knee.

"They're too long," He said.

"No they're perfect."

He pushed his feet into the shoes. They were the best thing of the outfit, not too high and wide. They were little girls' shoes and this wasn't good. He went to leave the room.

"Not so fast, sissy girl." Ellen was standing firm behind him, arms folded.

What now, he thought?

Ellen had a brush in her hand and two pink ribbons. She took the side of his long blond hair and brushed it through.

"Your look isn't finished yet, girly." She pulled the hair on the side of his head together in a single side ponytail. She twisted a pink elasticated loop to hold it in a ponytail. She tied one of the ribbons in a large bow. She repeated this on the other side.

She pulled all his hair into two long ponytails coming from the tops of both sides of his head. He looked like a caricature of a school girl. She finished the look by applying bright red lipstick.

"Now you're ready." She burst into laughter. "You look funny, Amy. I can't wait to see what the others think of this look."

David looked away to one side. It was one thing to wear plain girls' clothes. Now they were dressing him in increasingly ridiculous female child's clothing for their personal amusement.

Ellen shoved him towards the door and the stairs beyond. He dragged his feet to the first step. Dread filled his body at the prospect of his latest humiliation. A day dressed liked a cartoon version of a twelve-year-old schoolgirl, with large false breasts and the tiniest skirt he had ever seen. It was short and his cock cage hung below the hem, his penis visible through the bars. It was more like a frilly belt.

His phone screen lit.

It caught Ellen's eye. She stopped behind him and spun round.

Oh shit, he thought, my phone. He should have switched it off and now had to think quickly in case they took it away. He wanted to find out what Jennifer Strong wanted and who the lady was with the same surname was.

Ellen spotted his phone on the bedside unit, the screen alight. She strode over and picked it up. She read there was a message from Jennifer

Strong before it faded from the screen. She tried to open it, but it was locked.

"Who's Jennifer Strong and why is she confirming she will call you at 6.15pm this evening?"

This was not good. He tried to think fast. "She's an old friend, Mistress, she wants to catch up on news."

He wasn't sure he was a good liar. Ellen hummed a grunt. "I'll take your phone and discuss this with Louise. I'm not sure a sissy like you should have any rights or friends. Unless they are other sissies of course." She considered this for a moment. "That might be fun."

This was a disaster, the phone was his only contact with the outside world. He had lost all his rights; he belonged to these women. His penis tried to expand against the small cock cage. This was a bad sign too. It showed that somewhere inside him, in a physiological way, he was enjoying the current situation.

He was locked down and unable to go anywhere thanks to the COVID-19 crisis and he was serving entirely at their pleasure and amusement. Now he'd lost his phone.

6 – Sissy photo shoot

His phone went to the back of his mind when he entered the kitchen where the three ladies were waiting for him. He walked in and Jenny burst into gales of laughter at his new appearance. Jenny got up with her phone.

"I have to take shots of Amy the schoolgirl to send you my *bestie* friends. They will die with laughter at this."

David backed away. Ellen pushed him further into the room. Ms Ryder shook her head at his latest humiliation; amusement danced in her eyes. Ms Lipman stood and walked around him. Her red glasses sat on the end of her nose, a silver chain looped from the glasses arms down and over her large breasts. She lifted his skirt to look at his cock cage.

"Excellent, excellent." She leant in and lifted it with a single finger. "Nicely squashed." She dropped it. "It'll soon be a more appropriate size for a boychik."

Jenny held her phone up and he put his hands over his cock cage.

"No, no, Amy. Pose for Jenny. I'm sure her friends want to see how girly you are today and they can't see if your body is closed. Now stand in a girly way. Look proud to be a sissy."#

David didn't care for the idea of Jenny posting photos of dressed as a sissy over the internet. Jenny had taken several of him feminised previously; did it matter if there were more? Would anyone recognise him anyway?

Jenny went down on her haunches and lifted his skirt and took a couple of shots of his caged penis. She stood back and told him to pose in a pretty way. A slap around his thighs from Ellen made him jump. He put a hand on his hips and thrust forward. Jenny squealed and snapped. She stood straight again looking to send the humiliating photos she had taken.

He wanted to rush at her, grab the phone, delete the photos. His body strained to move. He couldn't move, Ms Lipman and Ellen had a psychological hold over him. Not to mention the spanking he'd receive if he tried.

A swishing sound announced the humiliating photos going into the internet, to her friends and who knows where. Soon they would be sharing him as a sissy on social media with other friends. They would 'like' the images and laugh at them.

At least he no longer looked like a man. Or a woman. He was now a sissy. If anyone he knew saw them, there was a good chance they wouldn't recognise him. He didn't know many people anyway. Maybe his girlfriend, the Russian health worker? Or had she been Ukrainian? And what branch of health was she in anyway? She had been vague.

Ellen was talking to Ms Lipman. She was showing her his phone and they were talking together in hushed voices, heads close together.

Ms Lipman spotted David watching them and wagged a finger for him to go over to her.

David shuffled to her, head down. He wanted his phone back. Louise took the phone from Ellen and held it to his face.

"Tell me about what you use your phone for and who you speak to, Amy." Her red-framed glasses sat halfway down her nose and she looked at him from above them. She reminded him of a school mistress.

A pang of nerves hit David's chest; if only he had remembered to turn his phone off. Now he might lose his only personal connection to the outside world. And never find out what Jennifer Strong wanted or who Ruth Amey might be.

It would be best to brave it out. "I don't use my phone much, Mistress. I have one or two acquaintances, but no real friends. I use the phone for the news. I don't get a lot of spare time."

Ms Lipman didn't look convinced. She turned the phone over in her hands, thinking about what to do. She came to a decision. "Give me your PIN, Amy. I want to look at what you use it for."

"But, PINs are private, Mistress." David complained.

Ms Lipman stood, her cheeks flushed red. "Listen, girly, you don't have any privacy, that's gone. You're my property. You exist to serve me and for my amusement. Did you not understand?"

He mumbled, "Sorry Mistress". The situation was spiralling out of control.

"Bend over, Amy." She moved in close to his face, he felt her hot coffee breath on him.

He bent over, his bare bum cheeks exposed. Jenny sniggered behind her fingers.

"Ten spanks please, Ellen. I want to see her bottom cheeks red raw; she needs to learn discipline. This is the only way."

Whack. Ellen wasted no time as her palm spanked hard against his bum cheek. He lurched forward from the force and the sting. *Whack,* down came another spank.

Whack, whack, whack. Five more times. Ms Lipman told David to stand again. He stood, his bum skin throbbing and stinging.

"PIN?" She said.

"1 2 3 4," he said

"You are joking, Amy." Ellen's incredulous voice came from behind him. "You're more stupid than you look."

"A putz," Ms Lipman said as she typed in his pin code and the screen opened. She clicked on his search history first.

She read out his searches, "20 most embarrassing photos ever, 10 cute dog images and clouds that look like spaceships." She snorted in disgust. "Not exactly in-depth research is it, sissy-girl?"

She continued to swipe through his search history as he cringed at her flicking nonchalantly through his personal life.

"This is more interesting." She showed the screen to Ellen. David what was coming: the screen showed a site of sissy photos.

"Oy, oy, Amy. This is a nice surprise. So you like boychiks after all? Would you like to play with one?"

David spluttered. He found the idea of she-males intriguing since his experiences working here. "No, Mistress, I was looking to see what was happening to me. What you wanted from me." His body went hot, despite the sparseness of his clothing. He hoped his excuse worked, he didn't want them to know his interest.

She flicked through more of his browser history. "You've looked at a lot of sites, Amy, that's a lot of research."

He looked to the floor. "Yes, Mistress."

She handed him his phone back. "Take it. But I want you to find sites with sissies playing with each other. Blow jobs and anal sex. Tomorrow you can show me what you found and the ones you like best."

David was shocked. "But, I don't want to play with other sissies, Mistress."

She handed the phone to him. "Maybe you do, maybe you don't. I think you do. Anyway, it's not your decision though, is it?"

He took the phone and shot a glance at Ellen. They had forgotten his text message from Jennifer Strong. "No, Mistress," he said.

Ms Lipman sat back down, losing interest in him. "Run along and get on with your housework. Today I want the entire house spotless, and each toilet sparkling clean." She looked hard at him. "I'll be checking."

He curtseyed and went to leave.

"Not so fast boychick."

He stopped dead.

"You're not very feminine, so this afternoon Ellen will be giving you lessons in walking in heels and sitting like a delicate girl. After this, you can return to your room, rest for an hour, shower freshen up and get changed to serve the evening meal. I have another girly costume for you to wear for this evening. I'm looking forward to seeing you in it."

"Thank you, Mistress," he said.

This was working out. He would have time to take Jennifer Strong's call after the lessons. He remembered to thank Ms Lipman and left the kitchen, taking his phone back upstairs. He had a full day of housework. The idea of cleaning the toilets while dressed as a schoolgirl in a skirt too small to cover him was like a weird crazy dream.

It was also exciting. He had always preferred to be told what to do, to not have to think too deeply. In some ways, this was what he had wanted. He tried not to think what outfit they would make him wear this evening. It couldn't be worse than the one he had on now, that was for sure.

As he worked he thought about Jennifer Strong. Why was a lawyer contacting him and who was Ruth Amey? All would be revealed this evening. As long as he wasn't disturbed.

7 – The call

His calf and thigh muscles burnt. Ellen had put him in high-heeled shoes for the training session. She had made him spend the past hour making him walk up and down, back and forth. She taught him to reduce the size of his pace, putting one foot directly in front of the other.

She had placed a seat in the middle of the room. After a couple of lengths of the living room, he had to sit daintily on the chair and cross one leg over the other. He was getting worried and not only by the training. The session was overrunning. A large clock on the wall had crept past 6.05pm. Jennifer Strong was calling him at 6.15.

Ellen had introduced a bum swing into his walk, expecting him to wiggle his bottom suggestively as he walked. She said he needed to attract men now he was becoming a girl. He guessed she was taunting him.

Back and forth he walked again. He told her his legs ached, she swished her hand dismissively. He was still dressed in the schoolgirl outfit. He turned and walked again, one small step in front of the other. He wiggled his bottom from side to side, feeling stupid. His cock cage swayed below the hem of his tiny tartan school skirt.

The clock clicked onto 6.10pm. He didn't have much time.

Ellen told him to sit like a dainty girl again and cross his legs. He wanted to slump but knew she expected him to sit straight and erect. The clock ticked onto 6.12pm. If he didn't go now, he'd miss the call.

"Enough for today, Amy. Go upstairs, relax a little and shower and put on fresh makeup. I'll be up at 7pm to supervise your change into evening wear to serve dinner. All four of us will be eating tonight. Jenny and I will cook and you will serve us all in the dining room. We have a beautiful outfit for you tonight, I can't wait to see you in it. It's a surprise, I know you'll love it. If not, we will."

That didn't sound too good. The clock ticked onto 6.13pm. He stood and made for the door,

"Hey, stop."

Now what? He turned round.

"What happened to '*Thank you Mistress Ellen for my girly training*' and my curtsey?"

A lie was in order. "I'm sorry, Mistress, I am busting to go to the toilet. I forgot, I apologise and I want to thank you for training me to be a girl." He curtsied. Time was short, he needed to be as subservient as possible to avoid any further delays. He wasn't sure if he could make it upstairs in time in the high heels.

Ellen wasn't satisfied. He waited as if on the starting line for a race. She thought for a moment but waved him away. He shot out as fast as he was able in the high heels. He ripped them off at the bottom of the stairs and lunged up two at a time. He ran up the first and second flights of stairs in a rush and into his attic room. He threw himself onto the bed. His mobile phone was sitting where he had left it on the bedside unit.

The screen lit with an incoming call, the name Jennifer Strong flashed. He snatched and dropped it on the floor. It bounced under the bed and he could hear it vibrating against the boards. He got down on his knees as the buzzing continued. He scrambled under the bed, searching with a grasping hand. His fingers folded around it. He grabbed it and hit the green answer button at the bottom of the screen.

"Hello, hello," he blurted.

"Mr Amey?" A refined educated female voice asked.

He stood and walked to the bedroom door; he shut it with a light click. He forgot to answer.

"Mr Amey?"

"Yes," he shouted in desperation. He composed himself. "Yes. it's me Mr Amey. Yes." Stop blabbering, he told himself.

"Ah, good, hello Mr Amey. Jennifer Strong speaking. I'm from Arbuthnot, Willis and Strong: family lawyers. How are you, Mr Amey?"

Her tone was formal. "Yes I'm good, Ms Strong. What is it you're calling me for?"

"Yes, yes. Of course, straight to the point. Good, good. Anyway, the reason for my call."

He heard her take a deep breath. "We represent Ms Ruth Amey and she asked us to find you. We're lawyers," she hesitated. "I told you, of course I did. Well, we have a department for locating people for our clients. For cases such as wills and legacies and so on. You understand?"

David sat down on the bed, his cock cage protruding from the tiny skirt. How lucky it was a voice call and not Skype or Zoom. Ruth Amey asked a law firm to find him? Who was Ruth Amey? He shook his head. "Yes I get it, Ms Strong. But I don't know anyone called Ruth Amey."

"Jennifer, please. No, you probably don't, Mr Amey. She last saw you when you were two-years old."

This was getting interesting. "OK." He revelled in the novelty of her referring to him as Mr Amey rather than Amy. Or stupid sissy. Or boychik.

"Ruth Amey is Richard Amey's wife. Richard was your father's brother. Ruth is your aunt."

David thought for a moment. "I have an aunt? I didn't know. I didn't know my dad's brother."

"Mmm," said Jennifer Strong. "Unfortunately, your uncle died recently. Fifty.

Tragic. A heart attack. He worked too hard, I fear."

"My dad and my uncle fell out years ago and he never spoke about him. He did tell me his brother was a lying double-crossing crook."

"Yes quite. I have a different version of events from Mrs Amey, but never mind, Ruth doesn't blame you for your father's behaviour."

His father's behaviour? But his father had always told him his brother had cheated him out of their parent's, his grandparents, business. His father's brother had ruined him, his father always told him. Usually when he was halfway down a bottle of whisky. It was why they were so poor and estranged from the rest of the family, according to his father. The family were all cheats and liars. According to his father. So why would his aunt want to contact him? She wasn't a blood relative.

"Jen, I don't know my aunt. Why does she want to find me?"

"Jennifer," she said. "Your uncle, Robert Amey, and your aunt Ruth, had no issue."

"No issue with what?"

"No issue means they had no children, Mr Amey."

"Why didn't you say, Jen?" This was hard work, this Jen woman was talking in a kind of code. Posh people did that. It made them sound better than they were.

"Jennifer. Anyway, Robert Amey left a will."

"And?"

"And, Mr Amey, you are a beneficiary."

"And? What does that mean? *Beny, beny, benyfishary?*"

"Beneficiary." Jennifer Strong said. "It means your uncle has named you in his will."

Time froze for a few moments. He let her words soak into his brain.

"Does that mean I'll be getting lots of money?" His mind raced. Money, cars, house? Would he be rich? His head swam, was this a joke?

"Yes quite, Mr Amey. Robert and Ruth Amey were co-directors of their family firm, Amey Apparel Ltd."

"Theirs and my father's firm," David snapped. "Until they conned him out of his share." He sat up, the anger flowing despite the news he was in his uncle's will.

"Mr Amey, your father stole funds from Amey Apparel Ltd. In return for them not pressing charges, he agreed to sign over the company to his brother and wife."

"That's not true, they tricked him." He couldn't believe what he was hearing. Years of hearing how his criminal uncle had stolen the company from his father. She was saying his father had been the crook. It couldn't be true. Could it?

"Mr Amey, I can show you the proof at a future date, including the police files. For now, you're going to have to accept what I say."

David calmed down. He remembered the will. It didn't matter what the truth of what happened more than thirty years ago, he was about to become rich. He waited for Jennifer Strong to continue.

"Mr Amey, I want to arrange a video call between you, me and Ruth Amey to discuss the late Mr Robert Amey's will. You are the sole surviving blood member of the Amey family. Your uncle needed someone to hand the reins over to. And since him and Ruth had no children of their own, that person is you."

"I'm going to be running the family company?"

"Not exactly, not to start with anyway. Ruth Amey is now the CEO and is running the company. She will take you under her wings and show you the ropes, so to speak. Obviously. You get nothing at first. As the sole heir, you will inherit on Ruth Amey's future death. Everything; their fortune, the mansion here and the others in Spain and California. They were multi-millionaires."

David tugged on his small skirt as he tried to process the information he had heard. A shout came from downstairs, it was Ellen. She was calling out to tell him she was coming up in five minutes and she had a pretty new sissy outfit for him to put on. He had to close this call and put the phone on silent and away in the bedside drawer. Away from prying eyes.

"OK, Jen. what's next?"

"My name is Jennifer, Mr Amey." She said. "I'll establish a Zoom call for the three of us to discuss the logistics of what Robert has laid out about you in his will. Please send me your email by text and I'll send you the Zoom invite."

What the hell was Zoom, he asked himself? Never mind, he would Google it. And email? He thought he had a gmail account somewhere, but never used it. So much to do.

"I need to go now, but how about the same time tomorrow evening. For the Zoom call."

His mind raced again, *Zoom, email, run a company?* Things were rushing ahead like crazy; things he didn't understand. What would he wear, how would he hide his hair style, his clothes on a video call? He heard Ellen coming up the stairs. Time to close the call down before she came in and heard what was going on.

"Yes, yes. Tomorrow at 6.15pm. I'll send you my email address later tonight. I need to get to work now."

Ellen was on the second flight and getting closer.

"Bye, Jen, thanks."

He cut the call as he heard the 'g' of goodbye from Jennifer Strong. He flicked the phone off and slipped it in the drawer as Ellen opened the door. She looked at him for an instant and a shot of guilt hit him, he didn't know why. He hadn't done anything wrong. Or nothing wrong in his mind, Ellen might have a different opinion.

As it was, she didn't say anything. She was carrying a red dress. He saw large frills around the hem, but at least this time, the dress was long. He guessed it would be an inch or two above the knee. A wave of relief flowed through him: the dress would cover him and be less humiliating.

After that call, his route to escape was opening like a bright light at the end of a short tunnel. He was happy enough serving their ladies, it was the way they treated him that was poor. It was as if he was there also for their personal amusement. Dressing him like a prostitute and locking his penis up. Wearing female clothing hadn't been bad: skimpy humiliating clothes were bad.

"Hello, dreamer sissy." Ellen's sharp voice pulled him from his thoughts and back to reality.

Jennifer Strong and Ruth Amey would have to wait for a day. He had another evening of being the ladies' personal servant and focus of amusement. He sighed.

8 – A change of plan

David curtsied after serving the four ladies the main course. Ms Ryder's thin eyebrows raised. Jenny sniggered like a child after having taken more photos. Ellen was sitting next to her niece and was quiet. It was her who had dressed him this evening, after all.

Louise Lipman sat at the head of the table and wore an expression of intense satisfaction. She loved putting him in his submissive place, while humiliating and emasculating him at the same time. He didn't know what he had ever done to her. She gave the impression she enjoyed what she was doing to him and that was sufficient reason. It was nothing personal

This evening, Ellen had dressed him like a Spanish flamenco dancer. The female ones. He was in high-heeled black shoes and thin black hold-up stockings. Ellen had linked his shoes together with a bright metal chain, which was padlocked to the buckles of both of his shoes. The length meant he could step no more than six-inches at a time. Ellen said he needed to be more dainty. Small steps were, apparently, more feminine.

One side of his long hair was clipped back with a large red hair comb. The other side hung over a shoulder. His dress was bright red with a large frilly hem and frills on the sleeves and with a low-cut top. The hem of the dress was above his knee and cut away; one leg protruded, showing the black stockings

He cringed at his latest humiliation and wanted to hunch. Louise barked at him to stand straight and be proud of being a sissy.

The evening passed slowly for David. The ladies enjoyed themselves and became louder as they drank more wine. Ms Ryder loosened up and forgot her writing for the evening. She laughed along as Louise, Ellen and Jenny made comments about David's clothing and how pretty he looked.

The ladies finished their meal and left him to clean and tidy the kitchen and stack the dishwasher. By 11pm, he finished his work. His legs and feet ached and he wanted to go to bed and lay down. Being a sissy maid was hard work. He sat down at the kitchen table and put his head in his hands. He wanted to close his eyes and sleep. He hoped Ms Lipman would allow him to go to bed. He heard her calling him from the dining room.

He pulled himself up, tiredness aching his body. There was an attraction to serving and wearing female clothes, but the work was tiring, especially when your steps were restricted by a chain on your ankles.

He staggered into the dining room and curtsied. Ms Ryder, Ellen and Jenny were sitting at the table. Ms Lipman was pacing with the room. "Amy," she said seriously. "Good news."

He was sure whatever the news was, it wasn't going to be good for him.

He swayed on his heels, wanting to sit back down. She didn't appear to notice his tiredness as she continued. "I'm going to go back to my home to live. The lockdown will go on for a while yet, so I'm going to take a risk and drive home in the lockdown. I can't stay here forever."

Ms Ryder shifted in her seat. "And I need to concentrate on my next book. Ellen and Jenny are my assistants: you've become a distraction." Ms Ryder said

What did he have to do with anything? What distraction?

"Yes, Ms Lipman and Ms Ryder." He couldn't think of any other reply

Ms Lipman began pacing again. She grabbed a glass of brandy from the table without losing stride. What was she building up to?

She stopped in front of him. "You'll be coming home with me. To serve me at my home as Fiona says, you've become somewhat of a distraction here and she needs to get on with her novel."

He shrugged, "OK." He thought a bit more. This meant he would be escaping from Ellen and the obnoxiously childish Jenny. A smile broke on his face. That news wasn't bad after all.

"It will be much easier for you at my home. Don't think I haven't noticed it's a lot of work for you, cleaning and washing for us all day, serving and clearing in the evening." She put the glass down on the table behind her and turned back to him.

That would be helpful, the work was too much, he was constantly tired. He liked being told what to do and to not have to think, but this was too much. Having Louise to serve alone would make things easier.

"You'll have someone to share the load with." Ms Lipman's face broke into a haughty smile. "Oh my, that was funny. "Share the load? Things at my home will be easier for you. I already have one housekeeper. You'll love her. Her name's Polly. She's such a sweet girl, about your age." She chewed over her own words. "Yes, you are going to love *Polly*."

What was she on about? Anyway, she had another housekeeper? He supposed that would be nice, at least he wouldn't have to do everything. He immediately worried about what the housemaid would think seeing him feminised. He shrugged, it was one more humiliation.

"We'll be leaving tomorrow morning." Louise said. "I'm going to pick her up from my daughter's home en route to my place. Polly's been staying there while I stayed here.

"I'm sure you two are going to get on very well. I hope so anyway. If not, never mind, you'll become good friends and perform for me." She went dreamy. "I'd been looking for someone like you for ages."

What did that mean? His life was turning upside down again.

9 – The journey

David wore a short black pleated skirt, a tight metal cage locked around his penis and a blue medical face mask. His feet laid across the back leather seat of Ms Lipman's large silver car. His slim heeled black shoes rested on the seat. She had told him to keep his head down. It was early as they were not supposed to be out because of the lockdown.

The top of the milky sun peeked above the line of flat fields through the car windows. Ms Lipman was driving and they were speeding through narrow deserted country lanes. She wore a face mask in bright red. His phone was in a bag in the boot of the car. For once he had thought ahead and found his email address and texted it to Jennifer Strong earlier that morning.

"Lie down, do you want someone to see you? Oy, you're such a putz."

He didn't want that. He lost sight of the breaking dawn, his view became tree tops and empty grey sky. There were no aeroplane contrails crossing it like interlinked expanding cobwebs. Nothing except clouds and birds.

Ms Lipman told him she was keeping to the back roads to avoid the eager attention of the police. She was not sure how she could explain why she was out in the COVID-19 lockdown with a feminised man on her back seat wearing a skirt, stockings and blouse.

"The lockdown rules permit only one person per car and you have to have a damn good reason for being out. We're supposed to be in lockdown. But, I want to get you back to my home, I've always wanted two housemaids."

He wished she would concentrate on watching the road instead of throwing long glances back at his smooth shiny legs as she spoke. He manoeuvred his tight cock cage, struggling to find a comfortable position since Ellen had reduced the size further. His penis was bent in two.

"Can you unlock my cage please Ms Lipman? It's too small."

"Don't be ridiculous, it needs to be small to make your clitty smaller. I can't have a sissy maid boychik with a male-sized clitty."

"But it's uncomfortable."

"Nothing worthwhile is ever easy, Amy."

He opened his mouth and closed it again. This was a debate he had already lost. These were not normal times. A pandemic lockdown, made to look like a girl and now, a Mistress who wanted his cock smaller. This was not normal. Ms Lipman was enthusiastic about him becoming her second assistant. So keen, she was prepared to take this risk to get him back to her home.

Ms Lipman didn't care for silence. "As soon as I saw you I knew you were perfect material."

She glanced back again, David was concerned, they were touching seventy on the straight parts of the narrow road. He also didn't understand what she saw in him.

"Polly is such a pretty girl. Like you. She needs help around my house, it's big. And she wants a *playmate*." She stopped speaking for a moment. "I assume she wants a playmate." She grinned in the rear-view mirror. "I want her to have one."

He had no idea what she was gabbling about. Despite what he was wearing, he wasn't a girl. He wore the clothes because he had to. And she said the word *playmate* in a strange way, he watched her wide leer in her rear view mirror reflection.

David reflected that at least Ms Lipman wasn't a nasty person, not like the obnoxious Ellen. She thought putting him in a tiny skirt was somehow a caring move; she was convinced he'd grow to love being a girl. Or was that a boychik?

His clitty cage was made of thin metal bars spaced about half an inch apart. His folded penis was visible through the bars, pressed hard against the cool steel. She had reminded him several times it was the best cage available: medical grade. She believed this was a caring move on her part. He supposed it was in one way.

He fidgeted against the car seat. She heard the squeaking of skin on leather and her eyes shot into the rear-view mirror.

"Keep down."

If the tight cock cage wasn't enough, his bum felt full. It had a silicone plug inserted. It had taken Ellen a lot of effort to get it earlier, even with all the gel she'd applied. Ms Lipman wanted it bigger than before. A smaller penis and a bigger bum hole. It made no sense to him. A smaller cock cage, a bigger butt plug. Things were the wrong way round for comfort. He guessed what her reply would be if he asked her to take it out.

She had already said his bum hole will stretch in time and become looser and much wider. Apparently things would be more comfortable. She didn't know why all males didn't go through bum-hole stretching much earlier in life. David thought she had unusual opinions.

David worried about his bum being stretched. MS Lipman said lots of people do it; there was nothing to worry about and he would see it had benefits. What benefits? He was unable to see why she wanted his bum hole larger? What possible purpose would that serve?

They hit a pothole in the road, his bum rose in the seat and fell back. The plug went a bit deeper. He got an unusual sense of stimulation which sent tingles down to his penis. That was strange.

The car was rolling around corners and Ms Lipman flipped the radio on. She chatted over the top of the music.

"I want your hair longer and blonder," she said. She glanced back at him, her face radiant. "Down to your waist would be nice, with lots of flowing waves and curls. And long black eyelashes. That would be so pretty."

The hedgerows flashed past. There was no other vehicle around, but what happened if they got to a busy road? What if someone were to look into the car from a van or truck when they were at traffic lights?

He asked himself how he had allowed himself to get into the situation where he was dressed as a girl in the back seat. He didn't know what to do. He knew it was wrong, he should have been tougher. He was confused, he didn't have to be here. It wasn't as if he was physically imprisoned and chained up. He was psychologically chained. In reality, he was free to go should he choose to do so. He'd be homeless and without money. And dressed in girls' clothing. That was a snag.

He laid back, feeling the car's air conditioning gently blowing under his skirt and through the bars of his cock cage. There was no escape, he belonged to the whims of this strange alluring lady for now. He looked at the back of her head. He would wait and see what happened when they got to her home. It was the only option.

He put a hand under his head and gazed through the car windows to the silent cloudy skies. The birds were swooping, carefree.

He had an idea he was going to find out exactly what she wanted all too soon.

10 – Uncovered

David was being thrown back and forth across the back seat. Ms Lipman's foot was down and they hit over sixty-five miles an hour on the twisting turning country lanes.

The car lurched and there was a long squeal of rubber on the road. David fell forward and crashed into the back of the front seats. He flopped to the floor. His legs were in the air and his mini skirt around his stomach. His back fell against the central hump and the breath from his stomach escaped with a wheeze. The car stopped dead.

"Oh shit," Ms Lipman said through the muffling of the face mask, tight lips and gritted teeth.

David pushed himself off the floor and back to the seat. He tried to sit up to see what was going on. He thought they had hit a cow or a sheep. He hadn't heard a bang although she had braked hard.

Ms Lipman spotted his movement in her rear-view mirror. "Get down, schmuck," she said, her mouth tight, lips barely moving.

David threw himself down on the seat again. He wanted to ask what was going on, but he worried she might snap at him again.

The butt plug had squeezed out of his bum when he'd fallen off the seat and it was loose in his panties. He didn't know whether to push it back in or leave it. He pulled the hem of his little skirt down to cover the outline of the cock cage. He wasn't sure why he did that, it was a natural reaction. No one could see him, Ms Lipman was looking ahead.

The plug was uncomfortable, a flexible lump against his bum cheeks. He supposed this was preferable to it being inside him. He was sure she would have a different opinion later.

He forgot the butt plug problem when he heard the sound of footsteps approaching. They crunched towards the car in a slow methodical manner on the driver's side. They were slow and deliberate, closer and closer. A walk of confidence, a walk of authority.

He couldn't see a thing, Ms Lipman's driver seat blocked his view. He didn't like this.

Tap tap; knuckles rapped on the driver-side window. A click and the smooth electrical whir of the window lowering.

"Yes officer, is there a problem?" Ms Lipman's voice was different, soft and girly almost. Deferential. Guilty.

David gulped hard. Officer. This was not good.

"There are two problems actually, Madam." A young female voice, polite yet flat and officious. A slight muffle as spoken through the cloth of an anti-COVID mask. She made the word *madam* sound less than the term of respect it should have been.

David's stomach knotted. He pushed his body deeper into the seat. He prayed he couldn't be seen past Ms Lipman and the back of her seat. His legs were weak and his stomach twisted tighter.

"We recorded you doing 63.4mph on our speed gun." The flat female voice said. She sounded bored with a resigned superior tone. "You were proceeding along a 30mph zone. Madam." That use of madam as a pejorative again and the formal language. "Secondly, there's a lockdown. You will need to provide a valid reason for being out."

"I'm sorry, officer." Ms Lipman's voice recovered some of her assertiveness, despite the apology. "I didn't realise the speed. I'll be more careful next time. If I can be on my..."

"Step out of the car please. Madam."

David's chest felt as if it had been hit by a brick. He tried to mould himself further into the seat. Ms Lipman twisted to one side and unclipped her seat belt. His eyes caught with hers. Her seat-belt strap sprung back into the holder. She opened the car door and got out.

He could no longer see her although she had left the door open. He heard the female police officer ask for Ms Lipman's driving licence. There were footsteps, heavy and slow, crunching on road grit. These were on the passenger side of the car. The officer was still talking with his mistress by the driver's side. The dull thud of rubber soles on asphalt continued. Steady, sure and confident. Oh no, who was this?

David screwed his eyes tight. He squeezed his palms into tight balls, nails digging into the skin. The thought Ms Lipman had told him his nails were far too short shot through his mind. She wanted him to grow them long.

Tap tap. A different set knuckles on glass. This time the glass was the back door window. He opened one eye, praying against all the evidence there was no one there. A female's face was pressed against the window of the rear door. Her eyes were soft and serious above a dark blue mask the same colour as her cap. It had a black and white checked strip around it and a bright silver metal badge in the centre. The badge had a crown over it and a circular black area in the middle. He read the words in his head: *Thames Valley Police*. Oh shit.

Shards of straight blond hair fell from beneath her cap. Two large ice-blue eyes looked straight at him. Unblinking, world weary. "Get out of the car please, madam." It was a different female voice; the same flat tone with a similar authoritative manner to the first officer.

He didn't move; he couldn't move. This had to be a bad dream. A nightmare.

The face continued to press against the glass. "Now would be good, miss." Her eyes fell to his stockinged legs: long, sheer and feminine.

The rear door opened and the police officer stepped back. She wore a luminous yellow safety jacket over a dark-blue boiler-suit uniform. Her trousers were tucked into black military-style black boots. He sat taller, trembling. He was a man dressed in revealing girl's clothing. How the hell was he going to explain this? He hoped the mask obscured his less-than-feminine face.

The officer waited. He had to get out. David slid forward and out of the door. He placed his feet on the road surface, black Mary Janes on black tarmac. A gentle wind gusted his skirt and his hands pushed it down. The officer caught a flash of brilliant white panties. And the frontal lump of a cock cage frame.

A faint nauseous feeling floated in his head and nose as he stood; a morning breeze flapped at his light skirt. The sun was brighter and rising, mist was burning off the fields. On the other side of the car, Ms Lipman had recovered her confidence and was debating the rules of the lockdown with the other female officer.

The officer facing David was shorter than him. She had no makeup around her eyes. Out of uniform, he would never have guessed she was a police officer, she looked young and innocent looking.

Her mouth dropped as she took in the realisation he was a man in a mini skirt with long blond hair and stockings. The mask had failed to obscure his real gender. Her eyes flowed from his legs, to his skirt and over his body to his partially-obscured face. Her gaze hovered there. Ellen had done a great job, but his face and telltale Adam's apple remained masculine.

She looked back over his pink fitted tee shirt with puffed sleeves, over his eight-inch long pleated skirt, smooth shiny stockings and down to his shoes. It was as if she was unable to register what she was seeing. Her mouth remained wide open. She realised her mouth was gaping and closed it and swallowed hard. Her cheeks flushed, two red circles grew bright against her porcelain white skin.

David felt her eyes tearing into him. He looked to the sky, to the fields. A flock of dark birds swooped and swirled above the hedge line.

He wanted to fly with those birds. Something twanged inside his belly, like an elastic band breaking and flicking hard against the sides. The feeling shot down into his caged penis. It surged against the cool metal frame of the cage. His penis wanted to explode into life, to grow big, hard and firm. It wanted to be a raging erotic erection. He was frustrated, caged and emasculated and stared at by a gawking female police officer.

The officer blinked twice. She turned her head towards her colleague on the other side of the car, keeping her eyes glued to David.

"Sergeant Hedges." Her eyes remained fixed on David's skirt and legs. "You need to see this."

11 – A foam bath

David could not believe Ms Lipman got away with a caution. "Try not to go out again, madam," Police Sergeant Hedges said. "Especially when you have a sissy laying across the rear seat." She spoke with a straight face.

Ms Lipman had been speeding at 63.4 mph in a 30 limit and they were out in the COVID-19 lockdown. He was sure the two female police officers were going to issue a penalty fine or to haul them before the magistrates court. He imagined being in court when the pretty young officer read her note book. "We registered the defendant speeding at 63.4mph during the lockdown. When we stopped the car, we located

Mr Amey in the rear seat dressed as a bimbo sissy girl." David shuddered at the imaginary future.

Instead, the officers had become distracted by his appearance: short skirt, stockings, high heels and a cock cage. They had told Ms Lipman they had seen a lot of unusual things as police officers, but this was a first.

In the short time he had known Ms Lipman, he had learnt she could be manipulative. She had used the police officers' shock, and intense interest in his overtly feminine attire, to her advantage. And, ultimately to David's disadvantage.

Spotting their interest in seeing David as Amy, she invited the two young officers to dinner after their shift finished. She told them he would be serving them dressed in a pretty maid's dress with her other maid. That was news to him. As they were strolling back to their car, Ms Lipman had added, "Wear your uniforms, officers, she needs discipline."

David cringed as they laughed and agreed.

Sergeant Hedges told Ms Lipman to go home and not to go out again, except for shopping. She bundled David back in the car, calling out that he was what she had been shopping for. One boychik, feminine and cheap.

That made the two officers laugh.

* * *

David was sitting naked in a foam-filled bath in Ms Lipman's sumptuous six bedroom house in the upmarket area of the town. Darkness was falling outside. Ms Lipman hadn't followed the police officer's instructions exactly. She had called at her daughter's home first to collect her maid, Polly.

Ms Lipman had made them kiss each other on the lips as a greeting when they first met. That wasn't very COVID friendly but Ms Lipman said they had no signs and she wanted them to be close. How odd, thought David. Never mind, it was nice to kiss a girl again after all that time. His Russian, or was it Ukranian, girlfriend wasn't big on kisses. Just sex.

Polly was an odd girl. She was David's height with masses of bleach-blond hair, heavily made-up, long black false eyelashes, enormous tits, a tiny pink maid's dress, high heels and fishnet stockings. David's eyes were drawn to her suspender belt, which wasn't covered by the micro-length maid's dress. Despite Polly's overly feminine appearance and nature, David noticed her hands were unusually wide for a girl.

Polly and Ms Lipman were standing by the bath. Polly was wearing a white plastic apron over her pink dress. It was like a nurse's disposable medical apron and it was longer than her dress. She was scrubbing his back with a soapy sponge. Despite her bimbo appearance, or maybe because of it, he was attracted towards her. He enjoyed her attention. Maybe when Ms

Lipman wasn't around, and maybe if Polly liked feminised men, they might have fun. They would be spending a lot of time together, so why not?

Ms Lipman wore an expression that looked as if she smelled something bad. "You need to be spotlessly clean for tonight, Amy. We have two lovely young police officers arriving for dinner tonight and you two will be the show."

David didn't like the sound of that, although he was more concerned Polly had reached down into the water and had taken hold of his erection. She scrubbed at it without comment. He looked into her eyes which were shaded by her extra-long false eyelashes. They flicked up and down as Polly looked back into his eyes. She squeezed her eyes and her mouth in a tight smile and ran a hand around his balls. Yes, thought David, she's interested. This might work out.

"Stand, Amy," said Ms Lipman. "Polly will rinse you off."

He stood and the water and bath-foam slid off his smooth hairless body into the water. Ms Lipman leant in towards him and ran a hand over his legs and body. She cupped his smooth balls. She nodded, although her face was still full of distaste. Maybe it was his straining erection.

She told Polly to put hair removal cream over his entire body and to scrape off his hair. He was smooth but she wanted him soft and feminine.

The situation was highly sexually charged for David. He guessed it was for Polly. Strange Polly.

An exaggerated girl, but she had something interesting about her. A faint masculinity, which was strange as her body was anything but masculine. Especially her enormous tits.

Polly lathered soap into her hands. Ms Lipman breathed out slowly, it was as if she was annoyed. "Bend over, Amy."

He was momentarily surprised at her command until her firm hand on the back of his neck pushed him over double. His hands fell into the foamy bath water. A sharp pain shot up his bum hole. It faded as quickly as it appeared. David twisted his neck to see Polly had shoved her soaped finger into his hole all the way in one swift movement. She looked wide-eyed and excited and raised her eyebrows at him. She pursed her lips in the faint impression of a promised kiss.

"I asked Polly to make sure you're clean and fresh for tonight, Amy."

David's first reaction to the finger in his ass was he had an uncomfortable obstruction there. Polly wiggled her soaped finger around inside him and things started to feel different. This was a first and he enjoyed the sensation. She withdrew her finger rapidly; he expected a pop like a Champagne cork.

David preferred people who told him what to do, it made things easier. He had found it difficult at Ms Ryder's because of Ellen and the childish Jenny. Although, he hadn't minded wearing girls' clothing in the end. This was different. It was as if Ms Lipman felt she had a duty of care to him. She wasn't nasty, like Ellen; she was matter of fact. She didn't appear to believe making him into a sissy was anything out of the ordinary.

"Oy, we can't have this," Ms Lipman announced in her plummy middle-class tones, tearing David out of his thoughts.

She flicked at his erection with a single finger. What did she mean by that comment? Questions buzzed around his mind. We can't have this? His penis? What did she plan to do? How far would she go to make him into a compliant girl? Surely not that far?

12 – Pretty in pink

"Get out and get dried, sissy girl." Her eyes flew over his erection. "What we do with your little clitty is a problem for another day." She shook her head. "It's not feminine." She sounded disappointed. "I suppose it will shrink in time. If not I'll need to have a plan B."

He stepped out of the bath and Polly passed him a large pink towel from the heated rail. He dry himself while occupied about what she would do with his penis. His erection was not going to go down anytime soon, if anything it was stronger. David glanced at Polly and Ms Lipman from the corner of his eye. Louise may have been around fifty, but she had an attractive manner.

Ms Lipman snatched the towel away and threw it on the floor. His erection raged, the end red and swollen, the foreskin retracted. Polly stared, her eyebrows raised, lips pursed. She rubbed her thigh with a finger.

Polly stood to the side of David and wrapped a large fist around his rock-hard penis.

"I do not want you with this monstrosity of an erection when the two nice young officers arrive. It's not feminine." Louise shook her head as if she couldn't believe he should have an erection. "The nice young police ladies might want to play and I do not want you looking like this. Besides we need to put this back away in the nice little cage for now."

David was not keen on the cock cage. He lost the thought once Polly started to rub her fist up and down his erection. Her large fingers gripped onto his penis skin in an oddly stimulating manner. He knew he shouldn't like this, but the events of the day, especially the bath, made him desperate for a release.

The first rumbling along the shaft of his hard penis came within seconds. Ms Lipman leant away from him, an expression of distaste written across her face. Polly moved in closer and rubbed his penis harder and faster.

Ms Lipman looked as if she was sucking on a bitter lemon. This made it more exciting. David exploded into the glass container with a shriek.

Polly pulled at his penis as if milking on an udder to get the last drips out.

"Wipe her clean, Polly." Ms Lipman passed her a packet of wet wipes.

"Make sure you clean behind her sissy foreskin."

David blushed deeply as Polly peered closely and cleaned around the head of his penis. Ms Lipman grabbed his limp penis and inspected it. She grunted an approval and dropped it.

She took a tight hold of his flaccid penis again and pulled him roughly out of the bathroom. She strode along the landing to a bedroom along the passage, leaving Polly to clean the bathroom. The skin around the base of his tender penis stretched out like a sail. She pulled him into the room, her hand tightening around his penis.

Hanging on a single rail in the middle of the room was a pink satin dress, identical to Polly's. It was exceedingly short, flared from the waist with several stiff white petticoats under the shiny material. There was a small white cotton apron fitted to the front.

Laying across the top of a chair was a pair of black fishnet stockings and a black suspender belt. A pair of black patent leather shoes with four or five inch heels glistened in the light next to the chair.

"Put your new clothes on, sissy. The dress is of high quality satin, no low-quality dreck here."

He gasped but he expected nothing different. Her eyes glared at him like two enemy search lights as he hesitated. A small smile came to her face.

"Put the pretty dress on and the stockings and shoes. There's a good sissy boychick." Her eyebrows lifted, waiting for his answer.

"Yes, Ms Lipman," he said.

He went to the dress and lifted it from the railing. It felt smooth and light in his hands, feminine, sexy. He was amazed as his penis twitched in response.

"Hurry up, Amy. Stop admiring the pretty dress and put it on."

He quickly unzipped the back of the little dress and pulled it over his head. He hoped for a modicum of coverage; He was feeling exposed. It slipped on over his body like a glove. The waist clinched his body an inch below his chest. It was elasticated. It flared out from the waist. There is a wide circular flare of the dress.

David wondered why Ms Lipman wanted him in clothes that exposed him. wasn't clothing supposed to clothe you?

Ms Lipman spun him round and zipped up the back of the dress. It was more like a blouse with a wide frilly waist than a dress. Ms Lipman pulled the suspender belt around him and clipped it together. She helped him into the stockings. He fought to avoid another erection. It was futile as it surged to full hardness once again. It was the heady mix of the dress: soft and feminine, the stockings on his smooth legs and Ms Lipman's distracted superior demeanour.

Ms Lipman produced the dreaded cock cage. She told him she didn't have time to have Polly milk him again and tried to force his erect penis inside the metal case. He squirmed and it was painful. The pain made it softer and she shouted a triumphant yes and clicked the padlock into place around it. Trapped once again.

"Polly will show you your room. You'll be sharing."

"But Ms Lipman, I thought you had six bedrooms?"

"I do," she said. "But I want you two to become best of friends. What better than to share a room and a bed?"

He didn't know what that was all about. She was encouraging them. This may not be too bad after all. He hadn't had real sex since the Russian, or possibly Ukrainian, girlfriend. She gave a fantastic massage. And how had she learned to do all those sensual things with her hands and mouth on his cock? That wouldn't have been on the National Health Service. Anyway, she said she worked in the private sector.

13 – The calling

It was approaching 6.25pm and it was almost time for his video call with Jennifer Strong and his aunt. David sat on the end of the double bed in the pink bedroom he now shared with the attractive Polly. He was troubled, not by the idea of sharing a bed with sexy Polly as that was an attractive prospect. Nor was he troubled by Polly hearing about his good fortune. Besides, she was downstairs preparing tea and cake for Ms Lipman so she would not hear him.

Earlier in the day, David had received an email from Jennifer Strong with a link to the Zoom call. He kicked himself for not thinking about the main problem before: the problem that he was entirely feminised and had no male clothes to wear for the video call. He was in full make-up with a long blond feminine hairstyle and a short pink maid's dress. He had to do the call; he was not about to throw away a fortune. But he was not David Amey any more. He was Amy the sissy. They were expecting a man, how would he explain this? Would it affect his inheritance?

He looked at the time on his phone, 6.25pm, almost time for the call. There was nothing for it but to pull his hair back in a ponytail to hide the female styling and wipe off his make-up. It wasn't perfect but it was the only option. They wouldn't see he was in a dress, as such if he kept his face close to the camera. They would probably notice he had a pink satin top on.

He went to the bathroom and cleaned away his make-up. He pulled his hair back tight in a long ponytail. It was light blond but it would have to do. His phone alarm pinged. 6.30. It was time.

He returned to the bedroom, sat on the bed and pressed the link from Jennifer Strong's email. The screen flicked through to the video call. As it started, he spotted an option to mute the video. He clicked on it with a deep sense of relief.

Half of his phone screen filled with the image of a thirty-something slim lady with straight shoulder-length mousy hair, a pinched face and thin lips. That had to be Jennifer Strong. In the other half of the screen, he saw a lady around sixty: His Aunt Ruth. She was a serious looking but attractive lady. She had long dark hair and large dark eyes.

"We can't see you, Mr Amey," Jennifer said.

"Er, no, Jen. I cut the video," he said.

Ruth leant into the camera. "Oh no, David. I need to see you. Put the picture on." Her voice was neutral and authoritative.

David felt a heat in his cheeks. His aunt appeared to be as bossy as Ms Lipman. He guessed she wouldn't have become CEO of a company without being a tough woman.

"Do you mind if I don't for now. Please?" he asked.

"Yes we do, David." Ruth shot back. "Now, if you don't mind."

He gulped. Plan B. Phone camera in close. He clicked the video mute off.

"Thank you, David," said Jennifer."

Ruth leant back into the camera. She furrowed her brow and squinted. "Why do you have dyed blond hair, mascara and green eyeshadow David?"

"What?" he blurted.

He flicked his image to full screen. In his rush he hadn't removed the eye shadow properly and he'd completely forgotten the mascara. It was water-proof anyway. He flicked back to the image of the two ladies who were looking at him with stony faces.

He dropped his phone in his flustered state and scrambled around on the floor and picked it up.

"Why are you wearing a short pink dress, fishnet stockings and high heels, David?" It was Ruth again.

He choked and his throat closed. When he'd picked up his phone they had seen him from further away. He nearly dropped the phone again as his body heat rose by several degrees despite the short flimsy revealing dress he had on. His cheeks burned.

Ruth looked at Jennifer. "OK, never mind. Let's get on with this anyway, shall we? I don't have much time."

Jennifer Strong stared at the screen with her mouth open. She shook her head and stammered, "Yes, right, of course."

David didn't know whether to hold the camera close to his face and show his make-up or further away and show his humiliating dress.

"David," said Jennifer, freezing for a few moments as she realised his male name didn't match his appearance. She cleared her throat and read from a folder. "You are named as the future beneficiary of the company, Amey Apparel Ltd and the estate of Mr Robert Amey and Mrs Ruth Amey on the death of Mrs Ruth Amey."

Jennifer Strong looked at the camera. Her eyes widened and she looked back down at her papers.

"To benefit from this inheritance, Mr David Amey will forthwith, henceforth and thereafter move into the home of Mrs Ruth Amey. You shall be under her instruction and guidance until such time as Mrs Amey is ready to hand over full control of Amey Holding Ltd to Mr... "She hesitated once more on the word *mister*. "Mr David Amey. And to be clear. Instruction and guidance means you will follow every instruction Mrs Ruth Amey demands of you. Failure to follow instructions to her satisfaction means you forfeit the entire inheritance and all monies and the company will go to charity." She looked up again. "Do you understand, Mr, er, Amey."

He stared at her image on the left of the screen. "No." He wondered if she spoke English. Hence with and forth or whatever?

"It means you will move in to live with Mrs Amey at her Berkshire mansion until her death and you will do whatever she tells you. You will move in immediately in order to benefit from the inheritance."

"Immediately?" he replied.

"Yes," said Ruth. "I'll send a driver to collect you tomorrow morning at 8am. Text Jennifer your current address. Be waiting outside ready."

"I have a small problem, Ruth," he said. She was unfriendly yet wanted him to live with her.

"And what might that be, David?" Ruth said.

"Well," he started. "I don't have any appropriate clothing to wear." He looked to the floor, he might as well be honest, they've seen him now. "It's a long story, but when I took the job as personal assistant, my clothes were ruined and the only ones my employers had were female. They have provided only female clothes ever since." He looked with what he hoped were imploring eyes.

Ruth waved a hand airily. "Wait outside your home at 8am tomorrow morning for my driver. We will sort out details later. I'm not really interested in the mess you've got yourself into."

That sounded positive to David. Maybe. Despite her lack of warmth, he was not about to throw away the opportunity to become a multimillionaire. He'd do whatever was necessary. "I'll be waiting, Ruth. Auntie?"

Ruth harrumphed. "6.30am. Sharp. And that's my first instruction. Don't fail."

"6.30am?" David asked. Ruth cut the call. 6.30 it was.

His aunt was going to be hard work, but for the first time in many years, his entire body felt light and stress free; a massive stroke of luck had fallen onto his lap. He'd be free of his deepening feminisation. Finally.

At that moment, Polly arrived back in the room. "Ms Lipman wants us both downstairs to greet the two police officers. They will be here in a moment."

Oh no, first he has to deal with the present problem. What the hell does Ms Lipman have in mind for him this evening? It was going to be a long evening.

14 – It's the police

The two young police officers had not stopped laughing at David and Polly all evening. The two maids were dressed identically in short pink French Maid dresses. They had arrived in their police uniforms and remained that way through dinner. Polly had cooked and David served. Ms Lipman told David he had to curtsey each time he entered and left the room. Once dinner had finished and David and Polly had cleaned, Ms Lipman said it was playtime.

David had no idea what that meant. It could only mean bad news, he was certain. He stood next to Polly. They were similar height and build, Polly had big tits though and was slimmer. Their identical pink maid's dresses were low at the front. David's showed a flat expanse of bare bony chest. Polly's boobs were a mountainous bulge of straining flesh.

"Have you got your handcuffs, officers?"

Katherine, the sergeant, unhooked a set of chrome handcuffs from her belt.

"Would you be so kind as to cuff Amy's hands behind her back, Sergeant Katherine?"

What? This was going a bit far.

Ms Lipman appeared not to notice David's concern. The sergeant Katherine clipped his wrists together with a practised twist. She moved back round and admired her work. She folded her arms, the three white sergeant stripes on each sleeve were sharp white and prominent.

David's head swivelled to one side and the other. What was going on? "Ms Lipman?" he asked.

Ms Lipman put her fingers to her lips and let out a long slow, "Shhhhhhh." She turned to the other officer. "Emily, would you be so kind as to cuff her ankles together?"

"Of course, Louise."

David took a step back. Ms Lipman held him gently but firmly. Emily knelt at his feet and, with a similar practise twist of her wrists, she locked his ankles together. She returned to stand next to her sergeant, both ladies with broad grins.

"Let the show begin."

David's eyes flicked left and right, wide as plates. Sweat beaded on his forehead. "What? What's going on, I mean why? Ms Lipman, Officers?"

Ms Lipman put her finger to her lips again.

She went to a unit and pulled open a drawer. David was unable to see what was inside. She took out a slim cherry red butt plug made of a semi-transparent rubbery material. She had a tube in the other hand.

She walked to Polly and placed the two items in her hands. "Polly, dear, if you would be so kind and do the honours."

David's eyes flicked to Polly. The grinning officers sat on a wide sofa facing him. His eyes flashed back to the butt plug. Surely not?

Polly tugged his panties to his ankles before he could react. Ms Lipman shuffled him round until he had his back to the two officers. He stumbled in his heels; he had almost no movement with the handcuffs locked onto his ankles.

Ms Lipman pushed him down and his bare bum faced the officers. "You may proceed, Polly darling."

David felt a cool gel around his bum hole before a finger entering about an inch. He jumped and Ms Lipman pushed him back down. Next he felt a cold smooth object enter his bum. He jerked. It slid in smoothly and Ms Lipman allowed him to stand. The object felt larger than the previous plug she had inserted at the farm house.

Ms Lipman shuffled David back round to face side on to the two grinning officers. He was disturbed that his penis was fully erect and poking out below the short dress hem. He pulled on the cuffs behind his back.

"And now for the next item on the show, Polly will give Amy a sexy blow job."

"What?" David twisted his head hard and he pulled a small muscle in his neck

Ms Lipman nodded to Polly who got onto her knees. A demure expression of faint reluctance spread across her eyes. It didn't prevent Polly placing a wide hand around his erection.

"Look, Ms Lipman, Polly is a gorgeous, sexy girl and in the privacy of our room, I'm sure a blow job would be more than wonderful. But here? With you and the officers watching?"

"Shut up Amy." Ms Lipman folded her arms and stared at him over the top of her glasses. "Get on with it Polly. And make sure when Amy cums, you pull away a little so we can see it hitting your face and tongue. It's no fun if it all goes on inside her mouth, is it."

Polly looked up from facing David's erect penis. "Yes Ms Lipman."

Polly put her mouth around the end of David's erection. David jumped a little and inhaled with a start. He jerked again as Polly's tongue ran over the end of his penis. Her mouth descended further and to the end, taking it into her throat. Boy, she was good, he thought. Unable to move anywhere fast due to the handcuffs, he had no choice but to enjoy it.

The two officers looked on with eyes like wide dinner plates and mouths in round O shapes. They had never seen anything like it. A live sex show for their entertainment.

David wasn't sure he wanted them to see he cum, it had been humiliating enough the time he had inadvertently cum on Ms Lipman's shoes when he had first met her. All the time Polly's blond head moved up and down the hard shaft of his penis. Below his rock-hard erection, he looked passed his penis to Polly's enormous breasts below.

Slow and softly, her mouth moved over his erection, a slight scrape from her teeth and occasional flicks of her tongue. His penis twitched harder and it was as if all his juices were surging from his balls and to the end of his erection. Polly pulled away and opened her mouth wide.

A warmth enveloped David. The end of his penis bristled with thousands of tingling sensations and he burst across Polly's face. Cum streamed down her cheeks and ran onto her mouth.

"Suck it all clean from her clitty, Polly, there's a good girl." Ms Lipman's glasses were still perched on the end of her nose.

Polly pushed her mouth around the end of David's rapidly shrinking penis. She sucked and licked, her slurping sounds were the only noises as the fascinated officers watched.

"It's nice and clean. Get up, Polly, it's your turn."

"What?" said David.

"That appears to be your favourite word today, Amy." Ms Lipman said. "I suggest you change it to, *yes Ms Lipman.*

"You want me to give cunnilingus to Polly while you all watch me?" he asked.

"Well it won't exactly be cunnilingus."

"What?"

"Yes Ms Lipman. Now get down, take her panties off and get on with it."

David knelt down with difficulty in the ankle cuffs, Ms Lipman was getting annoyed at his questioning. His eyes run down Polly's thin smooth legs. Sexy. His eyes fell on her shoes. He hadn't noticed before, she had large feet to match her wide hands. Much larger than he would have suspected for such a slim girl.

"Sissy daydreamer?" Ms Lipman tapped a foot on the floor. "Take Polly's panties down and go to work on her clitty, there's a good girl. Same as for Polly, we want to see her cum in your mouth and on your face."

"What?" How would that be possible? Was Polly a squirter? He'd heard about that.

He put his hands in the elastic waist of her small panties under her dress and pulled them to her ankles. He lifted her dress and froze.

15 – The surprise package

A massive erect penis faced him, an inch from his nose. A small drizzle of pre-cum dripped from the end.

He jerked away and tried to get up. Ms Lipman's hand rested on his shoulder. "Oh no you don't, boychik."

"But mistress. It's a penis." David tried to keep his head as far as possible from the monster facing him. It must have been ten inches and goodness knows how wide. How on Earth could a small slim person like Polly be endowed with such an enormous cock?

Ms Lipman took the sides of David's head and it to Polly's enormous erection. David smelled a damp musky scent.

"Open wide, boychik, and show the two nice officers how you can give head to pretty Polly."

David didn't want to do this, the situation was beyond bizarre. Yet. Polly was pretty, attractive and sexy. He had never thought for a moment Polly was male underneath the big hair, pretty face and huge tits. Huge tits? How did that happen?

Amy, I won't ask again. Open wide and put the nice big clitty in your mouth, there's a good girl."

One of the officers squealed in excitement. David opened a bit and Ms Lipman pushed his lips onto the end of Polly's erection. A salty taste burst on the end of his tongue. He shuddered.

"Wider." Ms Lipman said.

He opened his mouth mechanically. Seeing this Ms Lipman pushed him fully onto Polly's penis. She put a hand on his jaw and closed it around the huge member. David's lips closed around it and he felt the pre-cum slide onto the end of his tongue. He gagged slightly. Ms Lipman moved his head up and then down the long rod of hard flesh. Polly gasped and rolled her eyes to the ceiling.

"Now on your own, Amy. And once Polly starts to come, move your mouth away to the end and keep it open to catch her cum."

David shivered and followed her instructions, moving his mouth up and down. His lips flowed over the smooth skin. He tasted more juices, they oozed from the end. More squeals sounded from the police officers, Polly's erection hardened further and Polly groaned. She was on the point.

David took his mouth off and kept it opened at the tip, He licked the end . Polly said 'yes, and shot a line of grey-white semen into his mouth. David closed his mouth and swallowed, the warm gel-like substance slid down his throat. A second jet hit him on the cheek. He opened his mouth and a third struck his tongue again.

He licked around Polly's shrunken penis like a small lollipop and swallowed the juices. He shivered again.

The two police officers stood and clapped. One whooped.

"You may remove the cuffs now ladies. I think that was a success, don't you?"

David wanted to wash his mouth out. Polly looked dreamy. David hated himself at that moment. Polly was attractive. Maybe the fact she had a penis wasn't the end of the world after all. But where the hell did those tits come from?

16 – Out of the frying pan

Polly was fast asleep and breathing deeply. David untangled her hand from his hard cock, pushed away the covers and slid out of bed. He checked his phone, 6.15am. In fifteen minutes his aunt Ruth would be outside. Lipman usually didn't rise until around 7 – 7.30, he had to be quiet.

It wasn't as if Ms Lipman was all bad, or he didn't fancy Polly, despite the additional appendage she had. It was all about the money. There would be plenty of other opportunities when he was rich.

He dressed silently into a small black mid-thigh skirt and pink sweater. He rolled on a pair of black hold-up stockings. All he had were heels they would have to do. He brushed through his long blond hair. It was thick and down his back. He guessed Ruth would get it cut short for him and find proper clothing. He shoved what clothes he had in his holdall. Apart from a toothbrush and hairbrush, he stuffed it with his female clothing. It would be a day or two before his aunt would be able to buy male clothing. To be on the safe side, he should pack all the clothes he had.

He threw the bag over his shoulder, flicked his face mask on, just in case, and took one more look at Polly sleeping. He turned and walked downstairs with his high heels in one hand. He got to the front door and opened it. Outside a long black car waited, idling. Grey exhaust smoke billowed in the cool air. The windows were darkened.

He walked towards it, opened the back door and slid in. Sitting opposite was aunt Ruth, a fixed cool expression set on her masked face. "Home James," she said.

"Home, James?" David asked. Maybe she had a sense of humour after all.

"That's his name." She didn't smile.

The driver turned and nodded. He wore a peaked cap and a blue COVID face mask. He pulled the car away and they rolled along the quiet street.

Ruth's eyes swam over David's stockinged legs and to his face and hair without comment or expression.

David stared ahead and tugged on his skirt. It was the longest one he had, mid-thigh, and he suddenly felt awkward. His cheeks burned at the sensation of his aunt's eyes on him.

Silence continued, From the corner of his eyes, he spotted her mouth crease into a faint smile as she inspected him. The sound of tyres roaring on tarmac filed the car. David's discomfort grew.

"They made me look like this, Ruth," he said without thinking. He had to fill the silence.

"Aunt Ruth. Or Auntie."

He looked at her. One corner of her mouth was raised.

"Oh right," he said. "They forced me to look like this, Aunt Ruth."

"Did they now?"

"Yes. I had nothing to put on and they made me wear women's clothes."

"Is that right?"

"Yes, Aunt Ruth. And they wouldn't let me cut my hair and they dyed it blond and they made me grow my nails long and they painted them pink and they trained me to walk and sit like a girl and made me wear make-up and lipstick."

"I'm sure they did."

David looked at her again. Her smirk had grown.

"Nice legs," she said.

"Excuse me?"

"Nice legs. Smooth and hairless. Like a girl."

"What? Thank you. I think, I mean, they made me shave them."

"I guessed."

"Yes Auntie. They made me."

"And you put up a big fight?"

Where was this going? Why was Aunt Ruth teasing him? "Well not exactly."

"No? And why was that?"

"I couldn't. I had nowhere to go. I was trapped and tricked. I had to do what they told me."

The car moved into the slip road of a motorway. David saw the driver's small dark eyes flicking in the rear view mirror at him.

"Trapped and tricked, were you?" Aunt Ruth asked.

He exaggerated his sad expression. "Yes, I was trapped there and they tricked me into looking and dressing like a girl."

"I see."

This was going round in circles. David didn't care for his Aunt Ruth's smirk.

"And you hated this?"

"Yes of course."

"Did you?"

"Yes and they called me Amy on account of my last name."

"Amy Amey." She chuckled once.

David opened his mouth and closed it again. This was going nowhere and he felt his frustration building at his aunt's lack of sympathy for his plight. He breathed in deeply to calm.

"When we get to your house, Auntie, I'd like to change."

"Really?

He opened his mouth again. It remained open for a moment. "Yes."

Ruth's smile wiped from her face and set serious. "I'm not going to call you Amy."

David let out a long slow sigh. "Thank you, Auntie."

"It would be calling you by your last name. It's not appropriate for a nephew."

This was better, clearly she had had her fun and now she was getting back to business.

"No. Thank you, Auntie."

"Nor is it appropriate for a niece."

"What?"

She smiled again, the smirk returned. She thought for a moment. I like the names of flowers and plants. If I'd had a daughter, I'd have named her Holly, or Daisy. Maybe Lily or Primrose." She went into thought. "Primrose. That's nice. Primrose Amey. It has a cute ring to it, don't you think?"

This was not going how he expected. He thought he was going to be learning about business. He had to raise this with his aunt Ruth.

"Yes auntie, if you'd had a daughter I'm sure she would have loved that name." That told her and closed her down. Now for the business in hand. "I'd like to know what your ideas are for me learning about the business."

Ruth nodded. "Yes of course. I was going to go through that once we got home but if you would like to know my plans, we can talk now."

This was good, he'd managed to move her away from her weird teasing. "Yes please, I'd like that."

She nodded again. "Good. Good." She sat up and looked him in the eyes. "I believe the only way to understand business is to start at the bottom."

This didn't sound good, it sounded like hard work. What if she put him to work in the warehouse lugging heavy boxes and driving forklift trucks. Or as a clerical assistant in an open-plan office. Not good. However, he had to think of the end game. Wealth.

"Ok auntie, whatever you say."

"Yes it will be whatever I say, if you remember the terms of the will."

He did. He had to follow every instruction or forfeit his inheritance. "Yes I remember."

"Good. My plan is to put you to work in an office."

Oh no, it's the open-plan clerical job. Boring.

"I'd been thinking about it and during our Zoom call the idea hit me."

David tugged on his skirt again and fiddled with the hem. He had a feeling of dread.

"I've decided that in order for you to start to understand how the business works, I'm going to put you in working for one of my managers. She's a rising star and knows the business inside out. She takes no prisoners."

Oh no, another alpha female to deal with. He had to show willingness though. "OK auntie, that sounds a good idea. What will I be doing? Executive assistant? Assistant manager? Production manager?"

Her smile returned again. "Not exactly. She's the Marketing manager for Amey Apparel Ltd. Amanda Sharpe. A smart cookie."

This was like pulling blood from a stone. "What exactly will I be doing?"

"You'll be her secretary."

"Secretary?" he asked.

"Are you hard of hearing?"

Oh no, answering the phone and arranging meetings for a bossy woman. Was there no escape from dominant women in his life? "When do I start?"

"Tomorrow morning."

Aunt Ruth was clearly one for the minimum amount of words possible. "But auntie, that means we'll have very little time looking for a new wardrobe of male clothing and getting my hair cut and restyled and so on."

"Why?"

What did she mean by why? "Because I can't go to your office looking like this, can I?"

"Why ever not?" Ruth looked down at her phone and began typing. She pressed send. "There, done."

"What's done? What's going on?"

Ruth raised an eyebrow. "When you get to reception tomorrow morning, ask for Amanda Sharpe. She'll be there. Some of my employees are still working at the office during the COVID crisis."

"OK."

Ruth leaned in to David. "Reception will be expecting you, so when you get there, tell them Primrose Amey is reporting for work."

END OF BOOK 2

***Lockdown Feminization 3* will be out in early 2021.**

Here's an excerpt from the up-coming final book in the series Lockdown Feminization and the feminisation saga of David Amey.

David sat and rested his hands on the top of his light mini skirt. His long pink glossy nails were bright against the white flared cotton. His aunt had insisted on four-inch heels and a pretty shoulder bag which he placed by his side on the black leather sofa in the reception area of Amey Apparel Ltd.

He adjusted his pink medical-style face mask and crossed his legs. The sheen of his tan stockings glistened in the low morning sunlight pouring through the all-glass walls. Mercifully, the streets outside were quiet.

A lanyard hung around his neck and over his pink blouse with a frilly detail under the dark fitted jacket. A laminated credit-card like security badge hung from the lanyard. It said GUEST.

He looked to the floor, avoiding eye contact and the risk of being spotted as a man. That situation was not going to last.

Clipping urgent footsteps approached him and stopped, blocking the sunlight and casting a long shadow across him. He looked up. A tall lady in a dark suit and shoulder-length dark-brown hair was looking down on him. He swallowed hard. She put out a hand and a strained smile.

"And you'll be Primrose, I presume."

More books available from Lady Alexa

Lockdown Feminization 1

David becomes trapped by the Corona Virus lockdown at the isolated home of the world-famous author, Fiona, F L, Ryder. Unable to get back following an interview as personal assistant, he becomes trapped with just the clothes he is wearing when the lockdown comes into force the next morning.

Since he's trapped there and with Ms Ryder facing an urgent deadline for her latest novel, she gives him a trial. However, Ellen, F L Ryder's other employee, wanted the role for her young niece. Ellen therefore uses his enforced confinement, and Fiona's focus on her latest book, to try to drive David into failing at his job by making his life difficult. She undermines him by gradually forcing him into increasingly feminine clothing and styles.

Ms Ryder is distracted by her book and is uninterested in what she considers his petty complaints about Ellen's behaviour and his increasing feminisation. Slowly, but surely, Ellen turns the screw of his feminisation and humiliation.

A Sissy Cuckold Husband Book1 and Book 2

In book 1 we meet Karlene Adair who is a dominatrix to the rich and famous. Her reason to be is turning powerful males into submissive obedient sissies. When she is rejected by a wealthy businessman Paul Paige, a former boyfriend, she plots revenge. She enlists his wife, the former super model, Gemma Paige, to turn him into a little sissy girl and to cuckold him with a 6ft 4in body builder.

Despite their love, Gemma was frustrated by her husband's small dick and his below-par performance in bed. She throws herself into the task of feminising and cuckolding her husband with relish, under the guidance of Mistress Karlene.

In book 2, we follow Pansy Paul's wife, Gemma, the former supermodel who decides to turn her husband into a sissy. Again. Paul Paige is her unsuspecting husband, loving, kind and successful. Unfortunately for Gemma, he's also short, skinny and not well-endowed. Dr Fiona Boleyn-Hunter is a specialist in her field: male feminization. Paul's fate is set.

Gemma is frustrated at her husband, Paul's,

performance in bed. When she catches him spying on her as she works out, she decides the time is right to return her husband to sissy servitude and to make him a cuckold, as she did in book 1 of this series. This time, she wants no back sliding. Her husband's transformation has to be both psychological and physical. Who better to help that Dr Fiona, the tall sexual principal of an out-of town institute for feminization.

Becoming Joanne the Box Set

Re-written, re-edited and updated, the three Becoming Joanne books now all together in one box set. In addition, there are previously unpublished prequel and sequel chapters to compete the entire works, following the journey of Joseph as he is gradually transformed into the bimbo girl Joanne.

Joseph was a misogynist, lazy, drunk whose wife has had enough. She enlists the help of her best friend, Melissa, to teach Joseph a lesson. Melissa puts him to work in her all-female law office. But Melissa has other plans for Joseph, taking to heart Julie's plea to transform Joseph. Melissa puts Joseph on a path to femininity. But Melissa doesn't just want him feminised. She wants him humiliated and as bimbo. Melissa is unrelenting.

Feminized and Pretty, Books 1, 2 and 3

In book 1 we meet Patrick, a weak and scheming husband. His wife, Elisabeth, chose him because she wanted a pliable husband to dominate. The gloves come off when she discovers his attempt to take her money. Her revenge is swift, quickly putting him to work at her company as the most junior office assistant, dressed in a tiny skirt. He has no escape as he has no money of his own, no clothes other than what he has provided and no where else to live. His humiliations pile up as she realises there are no boundaries to what she can do to him.

In book 2, Patrick's wife, the formidable Elizabeth Remington, decides to take his feminisation and humiliation to a higher level. She remains angry at his poor attempt to take her wealth. After Patrick's failed attempt to escape from his wife's clutches in book 1, he realises that feminisation has certain attractions after all. Elizabeth spots his comfort and acceptance and sets about putting him through a series of very public humiliations including being pegged and cuckolded. Patrick's acceptance of his feminisation is soon challenged by these humiliations and his wife's desire to make his feminisation more permanent.

In the final book of the series, Patrick/Patricia didn't think his enforced feminization could be made even more extreme. How wrong he was. Patrick/Patricia begins this concluding book of the series after just having had an operation to give him enormous 42DD breasts. His work as a waitress, serving a mainly male clientele, becomes even more humiliating as Elisabeth forces him to work in low-cut tops and tiny micro skirts.

Still his wife is not satisfied and wants to take him to even greater depths of humiliation and exaggerated femininity. However, one day while working as a waitress he meets Elena, an enigmatic woman who takes an unusual interest in him. His transformation into femininity is about to become even more complicated.

The Reluctant Housemaid

The book covers two forced feminisations for the price of one, each set twenty years apart.

Twenty years ago a young man finds himself living with his stepmother and stepsister after his real father is sent to prison, They are not happy at having to look after him and start a campaign to transform into someone much more to their liking.

Meanwhile in the present time, a lazy husband is confronted by his wife who wants him to do more in the home. With the help of a sexy neighbour, he is forced to become their housemaid. And a whole lot more for the neighbour who takes full advantage of his vulnerability.

Forced Feminization Bundles 1, 2 and 3

Book 1 is a bundle of seven forced-feminization stories for the price of one. This seven-story bundle includes updated versions of A Sister-Law's Law, The New Assistant and Feminization is Compulsory. There are updated extended versions of my web-based stories Email Domination, An Unusual Proposition and Office Domination never before available in book format. Finally the bundle includes Memoirs of a Sissy Maid, the true-life story of how a repressed sissy was encouraged to come out by his assertive female friend.

Book 2 is a bundle of seven forced-feminization stories for the price of one. Bundle 2 contains From Here to Femininity, an updated version of Lady Alexa's novel The Woman's World, about a male entering a female-only commune. It also contains A Perfect Life - a female boss lives and works with feminised men; His Breasts - a man's wife wants him to have large boobs; In Dresses and Skirts where a young man goes to spend summer with his aunt and female cousins. His suitcase of clothes goes missing en route and it's a female-only household. Maximum Humiliation sees a male finding himself exposed in public. The Feminisation Game finds a husband whose wife wants more than a game. Finally, Feminized and Pretty, The Sequel which was previously only available to lady Alexa's newsletter subscribers.

Book 3 starts with Maid to Serve where a married couple start work at the remote country mansion of an eccentric English Aristocrat, Lady Elena Capel-Clifford, and her daughter. These two women don't seem to understand the need for masculinity in their household.

The Female Species has a young man posing as a pretty female intern in order to steal a precious specimen from a powerful female-only corporation. He plans to return to his former male persona once his robbery is done, but what will the corporation's response be when they find out?

In The Office Transformation, a dominant female manager decides to punish a young male employee for making a huge mistake that cost the company millions. The punishment is not what he expected as he's pushed headlong into a life-changing transformation.

An Accidental Feminization sees a male model undergo a series of operations he hadn't asked for due to a hospital mix-up.

The Mother-in-Law Dilemma has a bossy woman who comes to stay with her daughter and her gentle sensitive husband. There can only be one outcome.

Finally, the The Secret Girl is a short story about a man who has been feminized by his wife but, up to now, only at home. He knows she wants a whole lot more.

Printed in Great Britain
by Amazon